Sometimes, when I'm listening to music . . .

when I listen to the Pixies, I feel like I could scream. I feel like my skin's coming right off me or something. I feel like a whole bunch of bones. It's like some music's got a direct line to my insides, and when I hear it, I go crazy all over, crazy and turned-on and hysterical and so different from the way I look to everyone on the outside that when I look in the mirror, I don't really recognize myself. It's like I want to have sex or kill someone when I feel like that, and then I think I'm pretty crazy and I can't ever tell anyone I have those feelings. Not Ted. Not anyone.

—from *Brave New Girl*

brave

[handwritten annotations:]
Sarah - JT Leroy/
Candy - Terry Southern
Venus in Furs - Leopold Von Sacher-Masoch
Valley of Dolls

NEW GIRL

Louisa Luna

POCKET BOOKS

NEW YORK LONDON TORONTO SYDNEY SINGAPORE

An *Original* Publication of MTV Books/Pocket Books

POCKET BOOKS, a division of Simon & Schuster, Inc.
1230 Avenue of the Americas, New York, NY 10020

ISBN: 0-7434-0786-5

First MTV Books/Pocket Books trade paperback printing February 2001

10 9 8 7 6 5 4 3 2 1

Design by Deklah Polansky
Photography by Warren Aftahi

Printed in the U.S.A.

for my parents

ACKNOWLEDGMENTS

Special thanks to Clement P. Joseph, Stephanie Tade, Liz Perle McKenna, Greer Kessel Hendricks, Perry Meisel, Zach Luna & Laura Erlich Luna, and the Joseph family of Yonkers, NY. I owe you all a lot of drinks.

PART ONE

Tracey says you're an idiot, you don't know anything, you're a kid, get the fuck out of my room.

Dad says don't do anything stupid, no stupid children I made, don't cry it doesn't get you anywhere, only you can get you somewhere, don't screw up and leave me the mess to collect after.

Mom says don't swear, don't go out with Ted so much, don't let people think you're filthy and fast, keep your room clean, do all your homework, make some friends who are girls.

I don't say anything and just leave, because it's easier.

Ted's waiting for me by the 7-Eleven, sitting on the curb, holding his skateboard. I walk up to him, and he looks up and squints because he's not wearing his glasses like he's supposed to.

I got two bucks, he says.

Cigarettes? I ask.

I got a better idea.

He stands up and kicks off on his skateboard and rides slow so I can keep up.

What's going on? he asks me.

Nothing.

You going home for dinner? he says.

I don't know.

You can come over if you want.

Will your mom be pissed? I ask.

He shrugs. He says, She'll be having her own party.

Ted's mom's a real bad drunk, and everyone knows it. That's part of the reason Mom doesn't like me hanging out with him, but it's mostly because she doesn't like me spending all my time with a boy. Ted's my only friend. We were each other's only friend in junior high, and I can't imagine people being any nicer in high school, so we're still going to be each other's only friend come September.

Nobody likes him because he's quiet and dorky and not really cute and maybe looks a little too delicate. Nobody likes me because I'm boring and don't say much and still dress like I'm ten.

It's superhot but you really can't expect anything else here in July. I hate walking around outside in this weather because I just don't stop sweating and the smog's really bad, and all I really want to do is lie down. But me and Ted keep going until we get to the Trader Joe's, and he tells me to wait, and he goes inside.

He comes back with a bag of chocolate-mint UFO candies, and we sit down on the ground in the parking lot and don't say anything, and we eat them and eat them until they begin to taste chalky and we're so thirsty we could die. But we keep eating them until they're all gone and we both feel like throwing up.

By the time I get home, the place smells like meat and onions, and I figure Mom's cooking steak. I go into the living room, and Dad's there drinking a scotch and asks where I've been.

I was out with Ted, I start to say, but before I can finish he's yelling, Tracey!

Tracey comes out of her room, and she's wearing makeup and a tiny little T-shirt that says Hostess on it and makes her boobs look huge. There's this guy behind her, with her, I guess, and he has black hair and black eyes and he looks sort of mean, but when he sees me he smiles.

What, Dad? Tracey says, sounding all sweet for her friend.

Is your friend staying for dinner? Dad asks, not looking at either of them.

Yeah. Mom said it was cool, Tracey says.

Dad nods.

Oh, Dor, she says, like she hasn't seen me in days. This is Matthew, she says. Matthew, this is my little sister, Doreen.

Nice to meet you, Matthew says, holding out his hand, smiling, and I notice that his teeth look like a bunch of Chiclets.

Hi, I say.

Is that all you have to say? Tracey says, all annoyed.

How are you? I say.

Pretty good, he answers, and he laughs a little.

My family's not very talkative, Tracey says, and then she laughs and makes herself sound real dumb.

At dinner, Tracey keeps talking, and she keeps giving me looks, like I'm supposed to ask questions and act interested, but I really don't have anything to say. Dad's actually speaking more than usual, and Matthew's saying some funny things I guess, and Dad's laughing, but he's really mostly tired like he is all the time, and I'm pretty sure he's on his third scotch.

Mom's smiling because she likes the boys Tracey brings home because they're all polite. I think they're pretty smarmy.

Are you excited for high school, Doreen? Matthew asks, and I'm caught off-guard because usually nobody asks me questions, specifically.

I guess, I say.

Don't be. It's dumb, he says. Then he winks at me.

I feel a little twist inside my stomach.

Then I keep eating, avoiding the steak because the smell of it is

making me feel sick, and Tracey keeps yammering, which is enough
to make anyone nauseous.

I was talking to this girl, she says, whose boyfriend goes to Cal
and he said that there was a really good linguistics . . .

Blah blah blah.

I look up at Matthew, thinking maybe he'll wink my way again, but he
doesn't look at me. He doesn't look at Tracey either, though. Instead he's staring down at his plate. His steak and potatoes and salad and bread are all separated. He reminds me of a little kid. Don't let the food touch.

I think maybe Matthew's what Henry looks like now. Except I'm
almost positive Henry doesn't have a mouthful of Chiclets.

How old are you? I ask Matthew, while Tracey's in the middle of
a sentence.

Doreen, don't interrupt like that, Mom says.

Say you're sorry, Dad says.

Sorry. How old are you, I ask Matthew again.

He looks right at me.

Twenty-one.

I don't say anything. Henry's twenty-four. Ten years older than
me exactly. Almost to the day. He was born March second, and I was
born March seventh.

How old are you? Matthew asks, and I'm a little surprised.

Fourteen, I say.

That's a great age to be, Matthew says.

You just said high school's dumb, I say.

Dor, Tracey says, kind of laughing, like it was a silly thing I just
said.

You're right. I did just say that, Matthew says. I guess I have mixed feelings on the subject.

Everyone laughs a little.

I don't get it.

There's a knock.

Yeah? I say.

Hi, Matthew says. Can I come in?

Sure, I say.

I'm lying on my bed, reading the playlist on this mix tape Ted gave me last year.

He opens the door and smiles, walks in and starts checking out the stuff on my walls.

You're a big Pixies fan, he says.

Yeah, they're alright, I say, even though I know they're the best thing in the world.

I like them too, he says.

I watch him looking at everything, touching everything a little bit. He keeps talking to me but doesn't face me. He just stares at my wall, my CDs, the little picture of Ted that was taken when we were in the seventh grade, which is so old now that it's curling in at the edges.

Is this your boyfriend? Matthew says, tapping it.

No, he's just a friend. We're not going out or anything, I say.

I don't even know if Matthew's still listening, so I just keep talking.

Everyone thinks we are, though, I say.

Like who? Matthew says.

I guess he is listening.

Everyone, I say. All the kids we go to school with, my mom . . .

Don't you tell them how it is? he asks, interrupting, and now he's looking at me like it's the most important question he's ever asked anyone.

No, I say.

Why not? he asks.

Because I don't care, really, what any of them think, I say.

He smiles really slow now and gives me a nod.

That's good, Doreen, he says. You shouldn't care what anyone thinks.

I don't have anything else to say, but he keeps staring at me. So I just stare back and make it a game for myself—how long can I go without blinking, and then I hear Tracey in the hallway.

Matthew? she says.

I'm here, he says loudly, still staring. I'm coming, he says.

Then he just turns around and walks out without saying goodbye, and I shut my eyes, and they tear because they're so dry.

Tracey's done some crazy things, I guess. She's stayed out all night without calling. She got caught drunk at her junior prom. She says she never became a real raver because all the ravers she knows are stupid. She's pretty stupid, though. I hear her on the phone sometimes, and I just want to rip the baby barrettes right out of her boy-haircut. She mostly kisses Mom and Dad's ass and then talks about how she owns them to her friends. She has a lot of friends. She always has boys calling her. Always has. She just can't wait to go to college in the fall so she can get out of the house and away from all of us. She hates me because I don't talk. She hates Mom because she's indifferent. She hates Dad because he's not really nice. She really doesn't remember Henry at all, but if he was around, I'm sure she'd hate him too.

We should start a band, Ted says to me, sitting on the couch in his basement TV room, drumming the coffee table.

I don't know how to play anything, I say.

Doesn't matter, he says. We can learn.

What should I play? I ask.

Bass, he says.

The best bands in the world have female bassists, he says.

I get to name it, I say.

OK, what do you want to name it? he says.

I don't know yet, I say.

We start making up a song we decide to call "Crackbabies," but basically it's all a joke and all we're doing is laughing so hard our faces hurt.

Then his mom buzzes down on the intercom they have built into the phone.

Ted, come up here please, she says.

Ted gets all tight-looking and says, Be right back. You can put on MTV if you want.

Then he leaves.

I don't feel like putting on MTV because all they play is trash. I sit there with my feet on the coffee table, looking at the fake-wood walls and the brownish shag carpet that always smells a little funny. There's this ashtray on the table that's in the shape of a bathtub with a woman in it. Ted's mom smokes. I think that's strange—the only people I see smoking are kids.

We usually hang out in the basement when we're at Ted's, because you never know what kind of a mood his mom's going to be in. He likes me to see his mom the least amount possible. I can understand why, because she's done some pretty embarrassing things in front of me, but I don't really care. I don't like anyone to see my family either.

The intercom buzzes again.

Doreen? Ted's mom says.

Yeah? I say.

Could you come up here? she says.

Sure, I say.

I walk up the stairs, and I can hear Ted's mom talking really fast, and I can picture Ted even before I get to the kitchen.

He's sitting there, slumped down in one of the chairs, not looking at his mom, not even looking at me when I come in.

I don't think I'm being unreasonable, baby, Ted's mom is saying. Doreen, let me ask you, she says. She's wearing a pink dress with big purple flowers.

Mom, come on, Ted says, all red and sad-looking.

Let me just ask her, she says, a little unsteady. Doreen, honey, let me just ask you this—you guys are both pretty young, even though you're mature for your age—I'm not trying to . . . uh . . . say . . .

She stops because she seems to be having trouble. She keeps shutting her eyes hard and holding onto the counter.

I'm saying, she says, What I'm saying is . . . I'm glad you're Ted's little girlfriend—

Mom, stop, Ted says, looking up at her, then to me.

Ted, just give me a second here, she says. I'm trying to think. . . . You're a real nice girl, and it's no problem when you watch TV here, but Ted comes home so late all the time, and it's not right for two kids to be out so late all the time—

Doreen, leave, Ted says, standing up, walking over to me.

Now Ted's mom gets angry.

You don't know, Ted, she says to him. *I* know, she says, her voice getting louder. *I* know what it's like.

Get out, Ted says to me, taking my arm, pulling me over to the door to the backyard.

Ted? Wait . . . Doreen, wait, you both don't know, *I* know, Ted's mom keeps saying.

Here, Ted says, shoving his skateboard against me. I'll call you later, he says.

I don't even nod. I just take the skateboard and tear out the door, running through Ted's backyard, hearing Ted's mom still screaming, You don't know . . . *I* know. I get around to the front driveway, and I can sort of still hear her, and I drop the skateboard and it slaps against the ground, and then I just go, faster and faster.

Sorry, Ted says later, on the phone.

Forget it, I say.

I can't, Ted says.

I hear him breathing on the other end, neither of us talking, and I say, I have.

Ted doesn't understand that you can just forget things when you want to. It's a game. Just think like a little kid does and pretend something. Pretend you weren't in the room or pretend it wasn't you or pretend you were just the table or something instead of a body. It's only frustrating when you want to remember something and you can't. I wish I could remember Henry, but I really don't. I was only four when Dad made him leave, when he was fourteen. Sometimes I make up things about him—my brother out there. Sometimes I have fantasies about him. He's really good-looking and strong in all the fantasies and he sweeps me up, and it's sort of romantic when I think about it. But he's in shadow or something, and I can't see his face, but he smells like cigarettes, not the way Ted does or any other boy I know does, more like burning wood. I wish I could remember what he really looks like, but we don't even have any pictures of him around because Dad threw them all out. I'm surprised that I even know he ever existed. I hope he's far away or dead and doesn't remember any of us anymore. I wouldn't want to.

My mother comes in with socks and underwear and shirts. She's opening and closing drawers and closets and talking at me, but I'm not listening.

What? I say.

Listen when I talk to you, please, she says. Then she shifts and holds up a green blouse and gets all bright for a second.

Why don't you ever wear this? she says, moonie-eyed.

I shrug.

Well? she says.

I don't like blouses, I say.

I can hear her wind up tight as a knot.

You can't wear boys' clothes forever, she says, sounding very tense.

I shrug again.

Did you wash your hair today, Doreen? she asks.

I nod.

You have to wash your hair every day. You have to take a shower every day. You're really not a child anymore, she says.

She's talking to me like I'm a homeless person or something. I shower every day because I don't like the way me or my clothes smell when I don't.

Tracey might be able to show you how to fix your hair nice, she says, soft now, still folding laundry.

Great, I think. What I really want is quality time with Tracey since she just has so many interesting things to say.

Doreen, Mom says, all weary, picking up a CD that is out of its case. Doreen, if you leave them out like that, they're going to get ruined.

She holds the CD like it's a dirty sock and says, Where's the case to this one?

I don't know, I say.

Well, you can't just leave it lying around like that, she says.

Actually, if you put it face down, it's kind of OK, I say.

Alright, fine, she says, like we've been arguing for *so* long and she's finally giving in.

I don't know why Mom has to treat CDs and things like they're little people.

If it gets ruined, she says on her way out, don't say I didn't try.

Then she leaves, and when I know she can't hear me I say, I won't.

I'm sitting in the living room with Matthew because Tracey's still getting ready. She gave him a magazine because I'm sure she figures I don't have anything to talk about with him. So I start flipping through one because there's nothing else to do. It's one of those dumb women fashion magazines that Tracey leaves lying around. Articles with titles like, "What Men Love" and "All About Orgasms." Of course Tracey reads this shit. She probably makes notes in the margins.

I look up for a second, and Matthew's not reading the magazine Tracey handed him. He's just looking at me. I don't know what his trip is, but he's really into staring at people. I don't think he does it to be rude, though.

Do you want a newspaper or something? I ask him.

He shakes his head. I look back down at the magazine I'm holding, but I know he's still staring. I can tell when someone's looking at me. It's like I can *feel* it or something. I look back up at him.

Do you want to read *this* magazine? I say, holding mine out, thinking maybe that's why he's staring.

No thanks, he says.

I start to read again, but I can't concentrate when I know someone's staring at me, and he's not being very subtle about it.

Can I get you anything? I ask, thinking maybe he wants a soda or something.

No thanks, he says. Doreen, am I making you nervous?

No, I say. It's just that I thought maybe you wanted a soda or something.

Or your magazine, he says.

Do you want it? I ask, holding the magazine out to him and now I'm all confused.

No, no, he says, sort of laughing, and then he stops all of a sudden. I don't need anything, he says. I'm just fine.

I nod for a second, and then I figure I shouldn't go back to reading the magazine since we've like, started talking. Normally, with the tools Tracey dates, I don't give a shit what they think. But it seems like Matthew's sort of a sensitive type, even though he's a little weird. Suddenly, I don't want to offend him or anything.

How's your friend? Matthew asks me.

My friend?

Your friend not-your-boyfriend, he says.

Oh, Ted. He's fine, I say.

I think it's kind of strange that he brought Ted up. I mean, he doesn't really know me, and he's never met Ted, and he's asking how Ted is. Mom and Dad don't even ask me how Ted is.

It's good that you have a friend, he says.

He's really into telling me what I'm doing right.

I didn't have any friends when I was your age, he says.

Really? I say, because it's hard for me to believe. He looks like such a scenester, like the kind of guy who's always had a bunch of friends.

Really, he says. Nobody liked me . . . everyone thought I was strange.

I sort of want to say, well, that's a big fucking surprise, but I don't. It kind of makes me feel good he told me that. I suddenly wonder if he's told Tracey that.

Did you get more friends . . . I mean, as you got older? I ask.

Not really, he says, when I got to college I did, But before that, no . . . except for my girlfriend in high school.

I feel like saying, well *that* counts. Why wouldn't a girlfriend count? I wonder if he's lying just to make some connection with me. Tracey probably told him I'm a big loser. He probably feels like he's doing something really nice.

Your girlfriend wasn't your friend? I ask.

Oh no, I didn't mean that, he says, real quick to clear this up. She was my best friend, my only friend. It's just that when we were seventeen, he says, and then he just stops, leaving his thought hanging like that.

I hate it when people don't finish their sentences. It drives me right up the wall.

You guys broke up? I suggest.

Yeah. We broke up, he says.

He doesn't say anything else. He just sits there and smiles at me, and I don't know what to say again.

Well, I'm sorry, I say.

Thanks, Doreen, he says. That means a lot to me.

Whatever man, I'm thinking. Glad I've made such an impact. He smiles at me more, and I don't even really think about it, but I'm smiling back. I guess it was kind of nice of him to tell me that what I said meant a lot to him. Even if he doesn't really mean it.

Sometimes, when I'm listening to music, when I listen to the Pixies, I feel like I could scream. I feel like my skin's coming right off me or something. I feel like a whole bunch of bones. It's like some music's got a direct line to my insides, and when I hear it, I go crazy all over, crazy and turned-on and hysterical and so different from the way I look to everyone on the outside that when I look in the mirror, I don't really recognize myself. It's like I want to have sex or kill someone when I feel like that, and then I think I'm pretty crazy and I can't ever tell anyone I have those feelings. Not Ted. Not anyone.

I find my father in the living room after he has just come home from work. My mother has made him a plate of crackers and cheese, and he's eating them loudly. He doesn't really look at me when I come in, and then I feel dumb, because I don't remember what I came in for.

Doreen, he says, what are you doing?

I don't know what to say to this.

Right now? I ask.

You're not doing anything with yourself this summer, he says.

Now I know I'm in for it. The next words out of his mouth, I swear to God, are, There's no excuse to sit around when you're young . . .

No reason for a capable young girl to do nothing with herself for three months, he says.

There's really only two months left, I say.

That's a lot of hours, Dor, he says. A lot of hours to be spent constructively.

Dad's all about spending hours constructively. He's efficient as all hell, Dad. He works hard, I guess, but I think he hates it, so he basically wants to make me work hard and hate it too, and he finds some kind of pleasure in that. He sells sporting goods. Not in a store, but in a company that sells sports stuff to stores. It used to be kind of fun because there was all this equipment around all the time, red four-square balls and badminton rackets, things like that. We weren't supposed to touch any of it but I would anyway, and I really liked the way it smelled, real leathery and new.

He stopped keeping the stuff at home when he stopped traveling around a few years ago. I guess he told his boss he wanted to spend more time with his family, which I personally find hysterical because whenever he's home, he looks like he'd rather be scraping his teeth against the curb than be with any of us. Not that I mind. Doesn't exactly keep me up nights.

I guess he's trying to give me a work ethic or something, but it's kind of hard to want a work ethic when the only person you know who has one is a complete asshole.

The main reason I hate him is because he made Henry leave. I don't know details because I was only four, but I think Henry just pissed Dad off for the last time and Dad told him to go. I also know that Henry was pretty crazy; he bit Mom once when he was eleven because she wouldn't let him go out with his friends or something.

I think they look at him like he was a fluke, a mistake-kid. They really avoid talking about him at all costs, like if they say his name, that'll bring him back, and they'd be angry because they'd have to admit that they'd missed him.

I don't even know if Dad misses him. Dad wants people to follow in a line. He sort of treats me like the son Henry never was. He's always telling me to take responsibility for everything, to figure out my life now and be brilliant and do something incredible. And it's like, Dad, I just graduated eighth grade— I'm not exactly ready to be the surgeon general. He likes the fact that Tracey's girly and has boyfriends and probably is going to marry rich. For whatever reason, she got the girl slot in Dad's head, while I'm the un-girl.

So I've pretty much stopped expecting life lessons from Dad, and I'm reminded of this as he tells me, Clean out the garage.

The next morning I go out to our garage, which is this room behind our house, sort of. I don't know why they even call it a garage, seeing that nobody parks their cars in there—they just use the driveway in front. The garage is such a mess all the time, and Mom and Dad go back and forth and try to get the other to clean it, I guess, but nobody ever does. Probably because it's such a pit.

I start by just putting junk in boxes—books and magazines and lamps and stuff that looks like it's been ripped out of a car. I don't know if this is what Dad meant by cleaning out the garage, but I don't really care too much. I guess it's something to do. Pretty soon I'm sweating because it's so hot—it seems to be getting hotter and hotter around here, and I picture it getting so hot that the ground has to crack open just so the dirt underneath can breathe.

Most of this stuff I've never seen before, and there's probably no good reason why Mom and Dad have decided to keep it, except that it's too much trouble to throw it away. More and more books, which seems strange to me. Mom reads whatever looks steamy on supermarket shelves, with titles like *Passion's Flame* and *Regretful Sunrise*. And all Dad reads is the newspaper and maybe a magazine, if he's feeling really daring. Point is, I've never seen them read any of the books I keep dusting off and sticking in boxes—*Moby Dick, Robinson Crusoe, Great Expectations*. There's also a giant road atlas and a dictionary. I'm not too big on reading. My head jumps around too much. I'd rather go see a band play. I wish I was a big reader, though. When you hear about people who everyone hated in junior high but then became a movie star or a famous writer or a Nobel Pulitzer winning whoever, they're always saying stuff like they were always in a corner, reading book after book while all the cool kids laughed.

I don't know. I've read *Catcher in the Rye,* but I can't even say it's my favorite book because it's everyone's favorite book. It's Tracey's favorite book, for God's sake. And I hate her for it, because she's always said she's in love with Holden Caulfield, but I know if she ever met Holden Caulfield, if Holden Caulfield had the courage to talk to her at one of the dumb parties she goes to, she wouldn't look at him twice because he'd be too skinny or too weird or he'd have too many freak-outs, and he wouldn't be some Calvin Klein type with a Caesar haircut and an eyebrow ring.

• • •

Later I'm standing by the window in the living room and I see Ted coming up the driveway on foot, and I'm down the hall and out the door before anyone asks me anything.

Hey, says Ted.

Hey. What's going on?

Oh, you know. Little of this, little of that, he says.

Ted always says that, and I never know what the hell he's talking about. We start walking around my block.

I saw Karen Percy at the 7-Eleven, he says. She was with a guy from the high school, but he looked sort of girly—not gay, but I mean he could be a girl, Ted says.

How did you know it wasn't a girl? I ask.

Because I heard him speak, he says, And he had a really deep voice, but he was really thin, you know, like girls are.

Well, did he have tits? I ask.

Not that I could see. But anyways, I caught myself, before he spoke, I caught myself looking at his ass, because I thought it was a girl's ass, he says.

That's pretty sexy, Ted, I say, and he punches me in the shoulder.

I always find myself in these kinds of conversations with Ted. He feels the need to share a lot. I guess if he stopped, though, I'd miss it.

Ted lights a cigarette and offers me one, and I take it. I'm not a big smoker, but Ted likes to, and I sort of like the way it looks on him, and on me for that matter. But when Ted smokes, it's kind of strange because he's so young-looking. He's been smoking for as long as I can remember. He used to steal them from his mom until he realized she didn't care. I guess that took the fun out of it. I remember once, when Ted was telling his mom to go to bed because she was tired, when she actually had just drank about a gallon of Jack Daniels, she threw a pack of her Merit Ultra Lights or whatever at him and told him to relax. I guess when you're as tired as Ted's mom is, you don't care if your kid smokes or not.

As we start to turn away from my block, I see a car pull up in front of my house. Then I see Tracey and Matthew get out of it, and I figure it's Matthew's car.

What are you looking at? Ted asks. Is that Tracey? he says.

I nod, and then I sort of crouch down behind a car, and I pull Ted down with me.

What are we doing? he says. Who's that guy? he asks, squinting.

Matthew, I say, and then I watch them.

I watch Tracey pull Matthew toward the house, or try to, but he's really not moving away from his car. Then she gets up close to him and kisses him, and something turns inside me, and I look down. When I look back up, Tracey's going inside, and the car is pulling away.

What's wrong with you? Ted says. You look weird.

Nothing, I say, and I stand up and start walking.

You're such a liar, Ted says, catching up to me. Do you like that guy or something? he asks.

Just shut up, I say. He's Tracey's boyfriend for chrissake.

So? Ted says. That could mean you see what she sees in him.

It actually means that there must be something wrong with him, if he likes hanging out with Tracey, I say.

So if he wasn't going out with her, would you like him, a guy like that? he asks.

I haven't thought about it, I say, and I know Ted knows I'm lying again.

I go into Tracey's room when she's not there. I've never done this before, and she'd have a fit if she found out. But now, for whatever reason, I go poking around her room. I look at the posters on her wall—all these British pop bands she likes, like Blur and Pulp, and I sort of like them, but when I think of her and all her friends driving around in someone's daddy's Lexus, singing those songs, it sort of makes me sick.

Her room is pretty neat and orderly and I start opening drawers, looking at her extra-small T-shirts and, from here, I can see into her closet, full of retro clothes and like, nine pairs of superhip shoes. Tracey's all about hip.

I go into her desk drawer, and I don't even know why I'm doing it. It's like I'm looking for something specific, but I'm not, I swear. I find her stash of acid—three or four tiny little tabs with hearts on them. I've never done any of that stuff. Everything is fucked-up enough; I don't see why anyone would want to make the whole thing scarier and Technicolor. I close the drawer at exactly the right time because Tracey comes through the door right after.

What the fuck are you doing? she says, her eyes all wide and angry.

I'm looking for my Sonic Youth CD, I say.

Which one? she says, a little chilled out, believing that maybe I wasn't rifling through her personal things.

Dirty, I say.

Why would I have that? she asks me, as if I'm crazy, as if I thought she borrowed my golf clubs or something. You know I hate that one, she says. Everyone knows that one's a joke.

You're such a music snob, I say quietly.

Oh, shut up, Doreen, she says, world-weary, like she's just had the toughest day.

Where have you been? I ask.

Why do you care?

I shrug.

You know, I mean, what have you been doing? I say.

What's up with all the questions, Dor? she says, reaching over, grabbing her cordless phone.

Out of all the things I hate about Tracey, number one might be how she and her dumb friends start the majority of their questions with "What's up with" dot dot dot.

Could you leave now? she says to me as she's on the phone. Then she starts talking. Hey, Matthew, she says, it's me, it's about four-thirty, gimme a call. Then she hangs up, and she looks at me, just standing there.

What? she says.

Do you really like this guy? I ask.

Why do you care? she fires back.

I'm just asking, I say. Do you?

Sure, she says, shrugging. He's a little weird though.

Weird how? I say.

He just says weird things sometimes, she says, leaning up to crack her back, which sounds like popcorn popping.

All of sudden, I feel pissed off at her, like she doesn't get anything.

Maybe he's like, a serial killer or something, I say.

Jesus Christ, he is not, she says, looking straight at me.

You never know, I say.

Would you please leave now? she says, getting tense, and I like it a little bit.

Or maybe he has some kind of disorder or something, I say.

Doreen, get the fuck out of my room, she says.

I leave, and I can't explain why I feel the need to be such a little shit sometimes. It gets old just watching everything.

I could've been arrested once, when I was twelve. I swear to God. I was with Ted. We were out too late for kids that age—it must have been past eleven or something. I'd climbed through the rectangle sliding window in my room, because Mom and Dad would've busted veins in their heads if they'd known I was going out that late.

I still climb through that window when Mom and Dad get pissed off for whatever and don't want me going out, but I used to do it a lot more. I'd mostly just meet Ted, and we'd just go to 7-Eleven for a Tiger's Milk Bar or something. Not exactly a dance party, but it was something to do. We'd just walk around and talk about nothing, and nobody would really be out except the high school kids, and we'd see their cars every once in a while, swerving down dark streets. We could hear them yell and sing along with whatever goddamn Young MC bullshit they were playing, all drunk off cases of Bud somebody got with his brand-new fake ID.

I was pretty scared, actually. Not of the high school kids, but just of being out that late. It felt real quiet out there, and you could hear every noise your body made. Your feet on the pavement, your jeans against your legs, your breathing sounds. I think Ted was nervous too. Now, we're both used to it. But then, it was scary. We were just kids, though. We should have been in bed.

This one time, Ted and I were out at the 7-Eleven, and we had some Tiger's Milk Bars and soda, I think, and he had his mom's cigarettes. And we walked around to the back, where it was all fluorescently lit on the back parking lot, the blacktop, where no one was, and where the light sort of tapers off where the Dumpsters are.

We decided to go out back, because the guy behind the counter is always looking at us funny, like we're stealing or something. So we're back there, and Ted lit a cigarette, and he offered me one, and I said no. I just took his matches and started striking them, one by one, watching the flame on the head catch and sparkle and then calm down, almost to nothing.

I really loved watching the fire. I can't say why. It was just something cool to look at.

I grabbed this piece of newspaper that had been rolling around the lot, and I lit it.

Jesus Christ, Doreen, Ted said, all worried.

I laughed at him, and I don't really know what I was thinking. I just remember holding the paper upside down, watching the fire chase my hand. Orange, then black—it was crumbling up in my fingers, blowing away with smoke. I watched the words, the headlines, the pictures being all eaten up. It made me happy. Then suddenly I was laughing like a crazy person, and the fire was spreading toward my jacket. I could feel the warmth of it a little.

Then Ted grabbed the paper from me and threw it down.

Are you crazy? he said, stepping on the burning news.

But it didn't go out. Bits of orange live ash and paper flew everywhere. The more he stepped on the fire, the more it seemed to grow.

I guess some flew into one of the Dumpsters, because the next thing we knew we saw this real thin, twirly line of smoke.

Oh shit, Doreen, Ted said.

I started laughing again. I just thought it was the funniest thing, I guess. The rest I don't remember too well. Ted grabbed me, and we ran and we thought we heard sirens, but it wasn't even in the paper or anything. I was a little disappointed. It wasn't any big deal. The fire didn't get anywhere past the Dumpster, really.

I half wanted to get arrested, to have Mom and Dad shuffle down to the Pasadena police station and watch them get lectured on parenting by the cops. I half wanted to spend a night in jail, to stand at the cell door, let my arms dangle between the bars. I wanted to scare them, to watch Mom cry at her little girl gone bad and Dad shake his head and be ashamed that he raised another wild one, just like Henry.

I wanted to be so bad you couldn't even look at me. But I'm not. I'm just any other girl in the neighborhood who hates her parents and doesn't talk back. If anyone saw me in 7-Eleven or walking down the street with Ted on his skateboard, they'd just think, There goes some girl. And that's if they thought anything. Maybe they wouldn't think anything at all. Maybe it would be like they didn't even see me.

I go into the kitchen to get some soda, and Matthew's there. He surprises me.

Hi, Doreen, he says, smiling wide.

Hi, I say, opening the refrigerator.

How are you? he asks.

Fine, I say. Where's Tracey?

On the phone, he says.

I nod and don't have anything else to say.

I like your shirt, Matthew says.

Oh . . . thanks, I say.

It's just a plaid flannel.

Aren't you warm? he asks.

I shrug.

I can feel him looking at me even though I'm not looking at him.

Do you like my shirt? he asks, real quiet, like it's a secret.

I look up. He's wearing a plain white T-shirt.

I guess, I say.

Would you like it? he asks.

You're wearing it, I say.

I could wear yours, he says. We could trade.

Matthew is very confusing to me. But it seems like this trade means a lot to him. He really wants my shirt.

Sure, I say.

He smiles, and then he pulls his shirt off, right in the middle of the kitchen. I see his chest and the tattoo of a small sun on his stomach, and I have that same twisty feeling inside me that I felt when I saw Matthew and Tracey kiss, and it makes my cheeks hot. I look away quickly so he doesn't see me looking at him like that.

Here, he says, holding his shirt out to me.

I stand there, shifting for a second.

I'll turn around while you change, he says.

He turns around, his bare back to me, and I pull my flannel up over my head and put it on the counter. Then I pull on Matthew's shirt, and it's tight on me in the front because my boobs are pretty big now and it's a boy's shirt.

Here, I say, holding out the flannel, and Matthew turns around and stares at me.

Not just at my face, but at my whole body. I can't look at him when he does this—I want to wrap myself up in a blanket or something. I'm warm all over now. I feel like I might start sweating pools, running down my legs and back, puddling on the kitchen floor. . . .

I knew it would look nice on you, he says.

Then he puts on my shirt, and it's a little shorter on him than it is on me, and then he lifts the collar to his nose.

It smells like you, he says. I like that.

I really didn't think I had a smell. I take a shower every day, and I never wear dirty clothes—I shouldn't have a smell. And how would he know what I smell like anyway?

Then I hear Tracey coming down the hall, and I leave the kitchen real quick, forgetting my soda, and I go into my room and shut the door and lift the tight T-shirt to my nose and just breathe real deep for a few minutes.

Got me a movie I want you to know, slicin' up eyeballs I want you to know, girl you're so groovy I want you to know, Ted and I are singing in his basement, smoking cigarettes and doing this weird polka around the room.

Ted trips over the shag carpet, which is torn up in some places, peeling off and edging up in pointed sheets. He falls and takes me with him and we both laugh.

You're so cool, I say.

Shut up, bitch, he says.

No dirty talk from you, I say, standing up.

If you're dirty, nobody'll fuck with you, Ted says, taking a drag, trying to look all old, but he still looks twelve.

You know what? he says.

What?

Do you ever think, when people have sex, that space is being conserved? he says.

What people have you seen having sex? I ask.

No, I'm talking about in general.

What people, in general, have you seen having sex?

No, no, Ted says. OK, let's say two people, for this case—a man and a woman are doing it, and he, whatever, say he's six inches long. And for however long—twenty minutes, an hour whatever, for some period of time—six inches of . . . *matter,* is gone, conserved.

He nods to himself and sits down on the couch and lights another cigarette.

How did you think of this? I ask.

I don't know, he says. It just came into my head.

Ted, you, like, need some hobbies, I say.

All I need is a good time, he says, snapping his fingers and winking at me. Hey, he says. What's the name of our band going to be?

What band?

The band we're starting, he says.

I haven't really thought about it, I say.

Well, Ted says, standing up, walking the straight tear of the dividing carpet. Is it going to be the somethings or just like, one word?

One word, I say. Definitely one word.

What's your favorite word? he asks. Your favorite word in the English language, he says. What is it?

I don't know, I've never thought about it.

You've *never* thought about it? he says, like I'm so nutty.

Well what the hell's your favorite word, smartass? I say.

Ted looks up, puffs on his cigarette, and says it like he's reading it off a marquis:

Daisychain.

Then he looks at me, smiling and proud.

That's faggy, I say.

I'm not suggesting it, he says. It's just my favorite word. *You're* naming the band . . . so name it.

I can't think of my favorite word. There's too much pressure.

There is a lot of pressure, he says. There's a lot on the line, Dor. I'm not going to lie to you about that. There's the *Spin* cover. . . .

I hate *Spin.*

Whatever, whatever . . . We'll tour with this name. There'll be pictures of me and you, smoking and drinking onstage, he says.

You don't drink, I say.

I'll have to start . . . we'll trash hotel rooms and scream dirty words at music award ceremonies . . . we'll be the naughty kids of rock, he says, on a total roll, but not seriously or anything, and he keeps talking into the fantasy, and I stop listening and I have to close my eyes for a second and hold my breath when I start thinking about Matthew earlier today.

Ted, I say, interrupting him.

What?

I got it.

What is it?

I look up at him and pause for a second.

What is it? he says again.

Crush.

We used to have this dog named Spazz, and when he got really old, he got afraid of people petting him. You'd reach your hand down to pat his head, and he wouldn't move, but he'd shut his eyes real hard and shiver, like you were going to hit him. I think, for him, it was probably like that feeling you get when your nose gets hit a little too hard and that weird warm pain takes over your face for a few minutes. That's kind of the way I feel when I think about the whole shirt thing with Matthew. Like I'm getting crushed from above, and it hurts in a way but it's also a little bit good.

I don't want to end up like Mom. I know this because, among other reasons, she's on the phone right now with her sister, my Aunt Shirley, and she's crying because she's misplaced some recipe. Mom cries at things like that. This kind of thing makes her sad, while she gets out-of-control angry at me for leaving the milk out, while she obsesses for weeks, years now, that all I wear is jeans and sneakers. I don't know if she expects me to wear white gloves and party dresses, but she sure carries on like that.

Personally, I can't see how she can act like Ted's mom is cracked when she's breaking down because she can't make honey-cured pork or whatever tonight. I mean, I've always known she's a little loopy, but really. She's married to Dad—I don't know how I can expect anything else.

I'm sure marriage can be just precious—I've seen it on TV anyway, but it doesn't seem like either of my parents get much out of it, especially Mom. She's a lot younger than Dad. When he was a senior in high school, she was in kindergarten, which is a disgusting way to think about it, but there it is. And now all she does is get all uptight about things that don't matter, but as soon as any real issue comes up, like how late I can go out with Ted, or where Tracey is going to college, or kicking Henry out, I'm sure, she just shuts right up and starts folding laundry and lets Dad take over. And it's not like I think she has any mind-blowing advice to give me or her input would just change everyone's life, but I do feel a little sad when I think that maybe she did think about important things a long time ago and she's sort of trained herself not to say them, not even to think them anymore.

I'm back in the garage, and it's hard for me to understand why all this junk has been kept around. I go through fabrics—the kind you make drapes out of or something. Mom doesn't make drapes. She doesn't sew, really. These yards of fabrics are really dusty, and they're making me sniffle and my eyes water. It doesn't help any that the sun is streaming through the little window of the garage onto me, and I think I know how bugs feel when you roast them by magnifying glass.

The air around here is thick and dirty. It leaves this film on you that takes about a thousand showers to wash off. And it's really hard for me to go to sleep at night. All I wear is a T-shirt and underwear, and I open my windows and just have the sheet on me, and still I turn and reposition myself about twenty times, and by that time my mouth's all dry and I usually have to pee again, so I end up getting up to go to the bathroom and drinking some water, and then I come back and start the whole thing over again. And when I wake up, no matter what, I'm sweating all over, my hair's sticking to my forehead and neck, and I'm so thirsty I could die.

Last night was bad, because I couldn't stop thinking about Matthew. I keep replaying us trading shirts over and over again. I didn't tell Ted any of it. This is stuff Ted doesn't need to know. Ted wouldn't understand. He'd tell me that I'm a dork, that Matthew's Tracey's boyfriend, that he's got to be some kind of pervert for making me take off my shirt.

I don't know. I don't think too much about sex. Maybe that's not exactly true, but my only experience of it has been like, hearing gross grunting noises from Tracey's room when her scab boyfriends stay over, when Mom and Dad aren't home. But that's not too often. . . . And it's not like I *like* it or anything.

Then there are kids my age. Ted and I went to this dance for about
five minutes at the end of eighth grade. It was pretty disgusting.
Some kids were dancing, sort of, and some kids were smoking bowls
in the bathrooms, but then there was this whole group of dumb kids
who were standing around in the back, kissing and making out.
Hands all over asses, and the way they were kissing—so much
sucked in air pressure—they looked like a bunch of lizards, a bunch
of scaly lizards or snakes or something, trying their best to swallow
the other person's face.

It didn't exactly make me jealous.

I keep folding these fabrics and the back of my throat is getting
really itchy so I start coughing, and I just end up going outside to sit
on the curb and air out. I take some deep breaths and look at the row
of houses across the street, which looks exactly like the row of houses on my street. Big windows in front, where the living rooms are,
and little tiny sliding windows for every other room. Pale paved
driveways and lawns with twirling sunflowers and plastic flamingos
and sprinklers sometimes, but there's always a drought in California,
it seems like.

I also seem to remember a bunch of kids running around the
neighborhood all the time. Little kids. Little fat kids, usually, but I
don't see them anymore. No one's on the street in July because it's
not very good for you. It's too hot to sit in the sun, and the smog really gets to your throat and your lungs, I guess.

I hate it here. I don't remember a time when I didn't hate it.
Sometimes I think I'm crazy because if it gets really quiet and I close
my eyes and stop breathing for a second, I swear to God I can hear the

words coming right out of my head: You'll leave, you'll leave. Strong, then calm, like waves. I clench my fists so hard when I hear them, so hard that my nails make sharp half-moon marks on my palms.

I get called into the living room because Aunt Shirley and Uncle Bill are here for dinner, all the way from lovely Commerce. It's not fair— Tracey's not even home, and she doesn't have to listen to their noise. I go in anyway, and Uncle Bill and Aunt Shirley give me hugs and wet kisses.

Hey, tall glass of water, Uncle Bill says to me. Did you sprout up another foot?

Then he laughs.

No, I say.

Uncle Bill is something like ten years younger than Aunt Shirley. Aunt Shirley left her first husband, Uncle Jim, because she was having an affair with Uncle Bill. Or I guess he was just "Bill" then. I can't imagine either of them doing anything so racy. Uncle Bill has one of those feminist-feminine hairdos—short on top, long in back—and he's always wearing these shirts with no sleeves, which show off all the hair on his arms, and you can see it all peeking through the neck. I've seen him take his shirt off, and his back looks like a rug, I swear. Anyway, he isn't exactly irresistible, so I can't really picture him sweeping Aunt Shirley off her feet, which would be tough anyway because she weighs, like, nine hundred pounds. You'd think that her weight would make her jolly, because I guess a lot of fat people are, but she always looks and acts like she just swallowed a big wad of gum.

Hello, Dorrie, she says, wiping the lipstick off my cheek where she's kissed me. Are you enjoying summer life? she asks.

I guess, I say.

Dad sits Uncle Bill down on the couch to watch some game, and Dad doesn't really look too thrilled to be entertaining. I think Dad thinks Uncle Bill is kind of an idiot.

How's everything treating you, Hal? Uncle Bill says to Dad.

Oh, alright, Dad says, keeping his eyes on the screen. How about you?

I'm pretty impressed Dad's keeping the conversation going. I feel sorry for him in a way—he has to pretend to like Uncle Bill and everything, just because Mom is sisters with Aunt Shirley.

Doreen, Dad says.

Why don't you go help your mother out? he says.

Yeah, OK, I say, and I figure he doesn't want me around for some reason, but I don't think it's because he wants to tell Uncle Bill any big secrets or anything.

So I go into the kitchen, and Aunt Shirley's cutting vegetables and Mom's putting brown sugar all over this pinkish ham. I look at it sort of sideways, and there's this gross, jelly shit dripping off the sides. Sometimes the idea of eating really makes me sick. Just the idea of that eraser-colored ham mashing around in somebody's mouth—it kind of makes me not want to eat at all.

Hi, pretty girl, Aunt Shirley says, but she says it kind of pissed off, I think, like it's really not something nice at all.

I get embarrassed because of it anyway.

Dorrie's just growing right up, isn't she, Kathy? she says to Mom.

Yes, she surely is, Mom says, still fixing the ham.

Why don't you put your hair up? Aunt Shirley says to me. It's getting so long, she says.

I like it down, I say quietly.

I tell her to put her hair up, to wear a skirt, Mom says, like I'm not in the room. She doesn't want to hear it, she says.

It looks like you're going to be tall and skinny, Aunt Shirley says. Just like your dad . . . What do you think about that? she asks me, and I just shrug.

There's something about how Aunt Shirley talks to me, like I'm still four or maybe a hamster or something.

Want a carrot? she says to me, and I laugh, thinking maybe I'll go run a few laps on my wheel now.

What's so funny? Mom asks.

Nothing, I say.

Always in another world, Mom says. And then she says, Did you want something, Doreen?

Dad said I should help you out, I say.

Oh, Mom says. Well, OK, here, peel these, she says, handing me potatoes. I take them and stand over the sink while Mom and Aunt Shirley talk, watching the shreds of potato skins fall like leaves into the drain.

Is she having boys call her yet? Aunt Shirley asks Mom, about me, I guess.

No, she's a little young to be dating I think, Mom says, which I don't get, because I know she thinks Ted and I are kissing, at least. And anyway, Tracey started going out with boys before she could read, practically.

Good thing you've already gone through it with Tracey. It won't be such a shock, Aunt Shirley says. I remember, she says, when Ellen was fourteen or fifteen, and boys started calling her—Jim and I just didn't know what to do about any of it, Jim especially.

I find this hard to believe for a number of reasons. First of all, my cousin, Ellen, also weighs a ton and has serious allergy problems, and she always has. I'm so sure the boys were just banging the door right down, with a box of Kleenex in one hand and a Big Mac meal in the other. Also, Uncle Jim didn't really seem to give half a shit about Ellen's social life. He was always telling her she was clumsy and stuff. It was pretty mean of him, now that I think about it.

The more Aunt Shirley goes on about how shocking it was to watch Ellen go on all these dates, the more I kind of think she's lying. I look at her for a second while she's talking.

It's just something you have to get used to. . . . I would have to calm Jim down about it . . . you know, his baby girl, growing up, she says, getting quieter and quieter.

I look back to the potatoes and keep peeling. I wonder if Mom believes her. I wonder if Mom's even listening.

Mm-hmm, Mom says, still looking at the ham.

And now, of course, it's the same thing all over again at Santa Barbara, Aunt Shirley says. Only I don't have to see it.

She's a big girl now, Mom says.

I don't think Mom buys any of it. I'm sure Ellen's just knocking all the guys dead at UC Santa Barbara, where everyone goes to class in bikinis and shit. I picture her in some class, fat and sneezy and sitting alone. I don't know who Aunt Shirley's trying to convince that Ellen is some goddamn supermodel.

But Mom doesn't say, Hey, Shirley, I think you're full of shit. She just nods and agrees and pretends to understand. She's just lying right back, because I know she thinks it's all a crock.

I hope I don't have to lie about my fat daughter when I grow up. That is, if I have a daughter, and if she's fat, I hope I have the balls to say, Yeah, so what if she doesn't date boys? It doesn't make her a leper or anything. She still might possibly be an interesting person. Maybe she's really smart or she sings nicely or she's the funniest fucking person you've ever met. Nobody has the balls to say anything like that. I think I will, though. I really think I will.

At dinner, Uncle Bill's eating the ham like he's been stranded on a desert island forever. He sort of looks like some kind of farm animal, like a pig or a cow or something. Dad's sipping his drink and not really talking, and Mom's listening to Aunt Shirley talk about something stupid. I'm just eating potatoes, which aren't cooked all the way through, so they're a little crunchy.

I can't keep it in order, Aunt Shirley says. There just aren't enough hours in the day.

Well, Bill, why don't you lend a hand in the garden? Mom asks, sort of teasing him, trying to be all coy.

Oh no, Uncle Bill says, laughing. He even stops chewing for one goddamn second. No, no, Kathy, he says to Mom. No, I'm afraid I'm all thumbs in the garden, and none of those thumbs are green.

Everyone laughs, and I'm thinking, Good Christ, get me the hell out of here. But instead of leaving I just keep poking the ham with my fork.

Doreen, come on now, eat something. Don't just play with it, Mom says.

I'm eating potatoes, I say.

Kid eats like a bird, Uncle Bill says, all red-faced and smiley. Not like her auntie, he says, and he kind of slaps Aunt Shirley's thigh. You'd never see her picking at a meal, he says, and then he laughs with his mouth open.

It strikes me that Uncle Bill has had a lot of beer to drink since he got here. I guess there are some fat people who are really into being fat and always joke about themselves and stuff, but Aunt Shirley's not like that. She never even mentions it. And when she has about twelve helpings, she always says something like, I didn't eat lunch. And I think, yeah, you didn't eat lunch and I'm Chinese.

Bill, Aunt Shirley says, looking down. She's all embarrassed now, and I can see that Mom's embarrassed too, because she's shifting into action mode.

Whenever anything's too damn much for Mom to handle, she'll start running around, vacuuming carpets that have been vacuumed a thousand times that week or dusting the appliances. And now she springboards to her feet.

There are other kinds of dressings, she says and darts into the kitchen.

She comes back about a second later and puts three other bottles on the table.

Now, Bill, I know you like the Thousand Island, she says, and the rest of us are sitting there, not really knowing what to do, except Uncle Bill, who's still shoveling it in.

Thanks Kathy, Uncle Bill says and helps himself, pouring so much mucusey dressing on his salad that I can't even see the green anymore.

Aunt Shirley seems to get over everything pretty quickly, or else she just pretends to, and she starts yammering about some other lame thing. I look over at Dad, who's looking straight down at his plate, cutting his ham, eating it very slowly. He catches me looking at him, and he doesn't do anything. He sort of half-nods and then his eyes drift somewhere next to my head.

It didn't make much sense to me, Aunt Shirley says, talking about God knows what. Then she looks down to Dad at the other end of the table and says, You ever hear of that, Henry?

And good God, is it ever quiet.

I know she was probably trying to say Harry, because that's what Dad goes by, or Hal, but Henry slipped out, which, in this house gets the same reception that something like Jesus Christ can suck my dick would get in a church.

Dad looks up and Mom looks down at the same time. They look like part of a cuckoo clock or something when they do that. For a second, Henry is here. He's at the table. It's really something how saying a person's name can do that. If he was here, he'd probably be sitting next to me, facing Uncle Bill and Aunt Shirley. He'd probably be laughing.

What do you think about that, old man, I bet he'd say to Dad. Then he'd start fucking shit up. He'd probably yank the tablecloth out or fling the rest of the ham at Uncle Bill or something. He'd probably light a cigarette right here at the table and blow smoke in everyone's faces.

I'm sorry . . . Harry, Aunt Shirley says, all fluttery.

Nobody says anything for a second, and then Mom says, The cake's almost ready, and she's off and running to get the dessert, even though nobody's finished dinner yet.

It's alright, Dad says, looking up at her. It's really alright.

Dad starts eating again, and that's Uncle Bill's cue, and then Mom comes back in with her cake, and she puts it down on the middle of the table, and it looks pretty silly and out-of-place next to the salad and the ham.

Everyone looks pretty chilled out. Well, Dad and Uncle Bill do anyway. Mom still looks a little tense, and Aunt Shirley looks all weird and pasty, like she could kick any second. I'm thinking how I would have laughed if Henry was here—I would've laughed right along with him. He probably would've chucked me in the shoulder or something, met my eyes with some look that said, Let's make them think we've *really* lost it, and then we would've laughed some more. I laugh just thinking about it.

Doreen, Mom says, all confused.

It makes me laugh even harder. I look at Uncle Bill's and Aunt Shirley's dumb faces, and they keep me going. I just can't stop laughing. I don't even try to calm down. I look down at my half-eaten potatoes and untouched ham, and I laugh at all the food on the table and at Mom's stupid cake.

That's enough, Dad says, getting stern, and I can see it in his eyes, but even the threat of him screaming, which used to put the fear of God in me, can't calm me down.

I get sent to my room without dessert for being such a spaz, but I can't say I'm heartbroken. I already felt like I'd been sitting at that table for about ten hours, so getting banished from a Severna family dinner feels like time off for good behavior to me.

I'm lying on my bed when Dad sticks his head in.

Shirley and Bill are leaving, he says. Come out and apologize.

I don't say anything, and I get up and follow Dad down the hall. There are too many voices in the living room for just Mom and Uncle Bill and Aunt Shirley to be there. Tracey must be home.

Getting excited for college life? Aunt Shirley says to Tracey as I come into the living room.

Yeah, I can't wait, Tracey says, smiling like an idiot, and I roll my eyes to myself when Matthew comes out of the kitchen, holding two sodas.

What about you, Matthew? Are you going to college in the fall? Aunt Shirley asks.

No, ma'am, I just graduated from UCLA, he says, and then he looks over at me and smiles before Aunt Shirley asks him other stupid questions.

He stands there and answers them politely, and he seems to act really different around adults, and Tracey even, than he acts around me. He gets all weird with me, staring at me and asking me questions and everything. I watch him holding his soda, which looks really small in his hand for some reason. He leans back now and then, shaking the hair out of his eyes, and for a second, I want to run up to him and push his hair away from his face for him.

How are you, Doreen? Matthew asks, and everyone looks at me.

It feels like slow motion or something.

Doreen has something she wants to say to her aunt and uncle, Dad says.

I feel all dumb, standing there in front of Matthew and Tracey, giving my goddamn public apology.

What did she do? Tracey says, half-laughing at me.

I'm sorry I freaked out at dinner, I say to Uncle Bill and Aunt Shirley, and they smile and nod, and I don't think they give a shit one way or the other. It's not like I punched them in the face or spit on their food or anything.

Then I turn to Dad, who's still looking at me, like there's something else I'm supposed to do.

So, um, goodbye, I say, and I hug them, and Uncle Bill smells like a brewery.

Then I turn around and go back to my room, because I feel pretty humiliated actually. I hate Tracey for standing there, laughing at me, and now I know Matthew must think I'm a big tool.

I put on Velvet Underground because I'm just in that kind of mood—all rainy day and opium-den feeling—and I lie back down on my bed and think of Matthew again. I close my eyes and listen to the music, and it sort of cools me down, as weird as that sounds. It starts not to feel so hot in the house, and I picture Matthew holding an umbrella because it's raining in the living room, and then I'm asleep.

• • •

I wake up all confused, with sort of a jolt like I've been electrically shocked or something. I sit up, and I see Matthew, sitting at the edge of my bed, looking at me. I'm all sweaty from falling asleep in my clothes, and I can't really tell if it's night or early morning. I don't know how long I've been sleeping.

Hi, Doreen, Matthew says. I'm sorry, I didn't mean to scare you.

That's OK, I say, wondering why the house is so quiet.

You were embarrassed tonight, he says, not asking.

Yeah, I guess, I say, and I sit up and hug my knees to my chest.

Your mother said you started laughing and couldn't stop, he says.

Yeah, that's just about what happened, I say.

So what was so funny? he asks.

I don't know, I say, shrugging.

Come on, Doreen. You can tell me, Matthew says, scooting up a little from the foot of the bed so he's closer to me.

I *really* don't know, I say.

Matthew nods for a second, kind of in a twitchy way, and then he laughs real quickly and then he gets all serious again.

You know, sometimes I'll remember a joke from a really long time ago and start laughing wherever I am, and everyone looks at me like I'm crazy, he says.

He looks back at me, and I guess I'm supposed to talk now.

Isn't that something, I say.

He laughs a little, in his jerky way, completely stopping a second later.

You really make me laugh, Doreen, he says.

I think, Yeah, Matthew, I can hardly contain myself when I think of all the good laughs we've had together. But then I look at him, and I can't even think meanly about him. He sort of goes out of his way to talk to me all the time. And his eyes are these globes—they could just suck you right in.

You still have my shirt? he asks.

Yeah, it's in my drawer. . . . Do you want it back?

No, no, it's yours to keep, he says.

Thanks, I say.

We both just sit there, and I'm really wondering where the hell everyone is. Not because I want to talk to any of them or anything, but it's just that every time I'm with Matthew, or I see him, he makes me feel like we're telling each other secrets or something.

What are you doing tonight? he asks me.

I don't know how to answer him. It feels like it's about two in the morning or something.

I don't know, I say. Do you know what time it is? I ask.

It's a little after nine, he says, without looking at his watch.

I'll probably do nothing, I say, or I might go out with my friend, Ted.

Your friend, not-your-boyfriend Ted? Matthew asks, smiling his Chiclets smile, and it's weird to hear him say Ted's name.

Yeah, I say.

Well, that'll be fun for you, he says. What do you guys do?

I really don't want to say, Well, Matthew, we usually begin our exciting evening by going to the Trader Joe's or the 7-Eleven to buy junk food and eat it in the parking lot, and then when it's time to get *really* crazy, we listen to CDs in Ted's basement.

So I just say, A little of this, little of that.

He smiles and nods.

I see, he says.

What do you and Tracey do?

Not too much, he says, putting his hand through his hair. We drive around and check out some parties—friends of Tracey's, you know.

Where are your friends . . . from UCLA? I ask.

He looks at me and says, A couple are around, but most of them have taken off. All moved away. Matthew gets kind of tense-looking for a second and then he says, They've all got these great new jobs, see.

Do you want their jobs, I ask.

Matthew snorts out a quick laugh.

No way. They're all consultants or something.

I still wonder what the hell Matthew *does*. I can't picture him pushing KFC or wearing some Ken-doll maroon tuxedo, taking tickets in some movie theater.

I'm about to ask him what he studied in college, but there's a knock at the door.

Come in, I say, and Tracey does, all decked out in this shiny, slutty blue dress.

She looks a little confused at me and Matthew sitting on my bed, chatting.

Hey, you guys, she says, all nice and polite, and I'm surprised she even knocked, come to think of it.

Hey, Matthew says.

I'm ready to go now, Tracey says to both me and him, like it's really important that we both know. Like she wants me to say, Shit, Tracey's ready to go now—somebody call the papers and bring the Lincoln around.

Let's go then, Matthew says, and he stands up. Bye, Doreen, he says, extending his hand.

I reach my hand out to shake his, and he grabs it like it's a bird trying to fly away and he brings it to his lips and kisses it lightly. I don't even catch Tracey's expression because all I can think about are his lips on my hand, sending this pulse clear down my arm.

They both leave then, and I hold my hand for a second. I feel girly, and then I feel stupid for feeling girly, and then I just bury my head in my pillow and scream for a few minutes, because it really seems like that's all I can do right now.

When I see Ted sitting outside Tower Records, he looks all weird, like he has to piss or something.

What's wrong with you? I say.

Nothing, he says, looking at his shoes, pulling at the rubber on the sides of the soles.

I sit next to him.

Do you have any cigarettes? I ask.

He gives me one and lights one himself, and he's not too talkative on the whole, which is pretty unlike him.

I got sent to my room last night, I say. I was like yeah, too bad, I *really* wanted to watch Uncle Bill stuff his stupid face anyway, I say, and I think it's sort of a funny thing to say, but Ted just smiles all fakely.

I know I do it all the time, but I hate it when you ask people what's wrong, and they say "nothing." I guess people do it because they don't want to tell you. Or they think you should already know—they expect you to read their mind or something, which is even dumber. It makes me want to say, Excuse me so much for not being a fucking psychic friend.

What's up your ass? I say to Ted.

Nothing, OK? he says, all annoyed.

Well, can we go in please? I say.

Let me finish my cigarette, he says.

It's too hot to smoke, I say, putting mine out on my shoe.

It really is too hot today, right here anyway. I can feel the heat of the curb coming through my jeans, and, as usual, I've been sweating since I woke up.

What do you want to buy anyway? he says, all disgusted, like I'm going to say Peter Cetera's greatest hits.

I'm not buying anything. I just want to look around, I say.

Ted should know that anyway. We never really buy anything. Sometimes one of us does, and the other will tape it later. Neither of us has too much money most of the time.

I don't want to buy anything, Ted says. Let's just go to my house.

I don't want to go to your house, I say, and it comes out sounding more pissed off than I actually am.

Well, I don't want to go in there, he says, pouting still.

You're such a goddamn freak, I say. Hey, Dor, I say, imitating him, let's go to Tower so I can sit on the curb like an *asshole*—

Alex Matten's in there, alright, al-fucking-right? Ted says through clenched teeth.

We're quiet for a second, and then I say, You could have told me
that first.

It's just, he says, it's just kind of embarrassing, you know?

Alex Matten's this dumb kid who punched Ted in the stomach
once, right outside of school. And a teacher saw everything, which
kind of made the whole thing worse. Alex Matten got in all kinds of
trouble and kind of became a hero, because he was this rebel or whatever. Everyone's got it all so backwards. Alex Matten's no kind of
rebel—he's just another dickhead bully who gets away with everything and looks cool in the end. I hate people like Alex Matten—people who just get stuff. Meanwhile, he's dumb as a post. It's a wonder
he mastered coloring inside the lines.

You don't need to be afraid of him, I say, and Ted gets all defensive.

I'm not afraid, Doreen, he says. I know he's not going to *hit* me
for Jesus Christ's sake.

Then why don't you want to go in there? I ask.

I just hate him is all, Ted says, sort of looking all sad and defeated. I just hate his stupid face.

So do I, but I want to look around still, I say, standing up.

Alexandra Stuart's in there too, Ted says real quickly.

Alexandra Stuart is just about the stupidest girl we went to junior
high with. Alex Matten's sort of dating her. It's sort of fucking disgusting. Alexandra Stuart's real pretty and everything. She's always
wearing these little plaid skirts that hike halfway up her ass every time
she takes a step. She's real skinny too—no tits, no hips, and all the
boys just love her. She's also as mean as they get. Her whole crew of
stupid skinny girls walk around like they own wherever they are.

I don't care what anyone says—girls are about a thousand times worse than boys. Boys will just punch you in the gut and get it over with. But girls won't even treat you like a person—they won't even give you enough *credit* to punch you in the gut.

Most of the time they ignore me, but sometimes they say things. It's sort of easier when they say things, because then at least I can roll my eyes at them or something. The worst is when I know they're talking about me—when they're sitting around the lunch table like birds, looking over at me and Ted every few seconds. Then I just feel on trial or something. I mean, I don't *care* what they think of me, but it just makes you think how soon people become assholes. It's not reserved for adults or anything.

I don't care, I say, giving Ted my hand to help him up. Let's go in.

So we go in. I don't see them right away, and then I do. Alex is there with his dreadlocks, which he probably paid a hundred bucks for somebody to put in, and Alexandra's wearing these tight corduroy pants with a baby T-shirt.

I *hate* baby T-shirts.

They're standing in the H-I-J section of Pop-Rock, stocking up on Jesus Christ knows what.

I look at Ted, and he looks a little too nervous, and I wonder if I look nervous. I start flipping through some CDs in front of me, not even looking at them really.

I hate feeling stupid. There's just something about some people that can make you feel so stupid. Just standing in Tower, minding my own business, I feel all stupid with Alex and Alex standing on the other side of the store. But I don't want to. I look over at Ted, and he looks like he's thinking the same thing as me, and I get sort of angry at him for that.

Would you stop being such a dork and just relax? I say.

I'm just standing here, he says.

And then Alexandra comes up to us.

Doreen Severna, she says, smiling, as Ted turns away and starts going through CDs.

Hey, Alex, I say to her.

Hi, Ted, she says, looking over my shoulder at Ted, who's kind of hiding, I think.

Hi, Ted says, barely looking up, sounding all weird and shaky, and then he goes back to the CDs all quick, like it's *really* important he looks through them.

What are you guys up to? she asks me.

Just looking through CDs, I say.

Obviously, she says, sort of rolling her eyes.

She had to say that and make me feel all stupid and about as accepted as a *hunchback*. And I know I should say something sort of rude back to her, but I just can't think of anything. I just stare at her for a second and notice that her lips never fully close. Her mouth is closed, but her lips are still a little open.

What are you guys doing this weekend, she says, and I can hear Ted trying to slink away.

I don't know, I say, looking at Ted for a second, who's pretending he can't hear us but it's sort of real clear that he can.

Nothing, I don't think, I say.

I'm having people over on Friday night, Alex says.

Having people over. That's what everybody says. Tracey's always asking her friends on the phone if they're "having people over." And then someone goes to get beer, and that person's "buying up." That's all anyone's about around here—having people over and buying up.

I can't imagine having much fun at a party with Alex and Alex and Karen Percy and Dave "suck my left one" Campos. He's really into telling people to suck his left one.

Do you have plans . . . or what? she asks, kind of confused, I guess. She probably figures me and Ted would have nothing else to do.

I don't know if I'm grounded or not. That's the thing, I lie.

Well, OK, she says, still puzzled, and I'm sure she thinks I'm a total dork, not knowing if I'm grounded and everything.

Give me your hand, she says, and I do and she takes it, and her skin's really soft. She pulls a pen out of nowhere and starts writing on the back of my hand.

Alex and her friends are always writing on the backs of each other's hands. It's like some kind of really cute thing, I guess.

That's my address in case you guys want to come, she says.

OK, I say quietly, and I just look at the address.

It's not going to be any big thing, she says, and I kind of don't believe this. I mean, she's treated me and Ted like we were midgets or something since day one, and now she's convincing me to come to her stupid party.

See you. Bye, Ted, she says, looking over my shoulder, and then she turns around and walks over to Boy Alex, who's at the door. She's got this really straight hair that comes down to a perfect point on her back, like a sword or something. I really wish I had hair like that sometimes, instead of the knotty, curly mess my hair is.

I turn around to Ted, who's pulling at my shirt like he's my kid or something. He looks all wide-eyed and weird, maybe a little excited.

What night is it? he asks, trying to see my hand.

Friday.

Ted takes my hand like it's the Rosetta Stone and stares at the address, and it's becoming clear that he really wants to go to this thing, which will be the most lame experience of my lifetime.

If I did go, I probably wouldn't say one word to any of them. Especially those girls. I really don't care what they think, but I know they think I'm stupid or dead inside because I never talk. Which doesn't say much for any of them because I'm sure all they talk about is lip gloss and bulimia.

I can't stand talking to them because I can't pretend all that shit's important. I guess Ted and I don't talk about important things either, but it's better, what we talk about. They'd probably think it was stupid. I really think people just go around their whole lives thinking everyone but them is an idiot.

Why don't you want to go? Ted whines to me on the phone later.

Because it's going to be so *lame,* I say.

So? Ted says. It's something to do, at least.

That's no kind of reason to go, I say. *Anything* is something to do.

Ted exhales really loud to let me know he's annoyed.

Then he says, You're telling me you'd rather sit at home and do nothing?

I think about sitting on my bed with Matthew all of a sudden when he says that.

Well? Ted says, like he's scolding me or something.

You're telling me you want to go to this lameass party and drink Sambuca out of Papa Stuart's liquor cabinet? I say back to him. That's all it's going to be, I say. No one's going to talk to us. It'll be just like school except everyone'll be drunk.

Then why did she ask us to come? Ted says.

I don't know, I say.

Can we just go for a few minutes, just to see? Ted asks, and he sounds so pathetic and small.

God, I say, and I think I sound like an old woman. You know, I say, you could go without me.

As soon as I say that though, I'm sorry I did, because I picture Ted at this party without me, and it's enough to make me cry almost.

Doreen, come on, Ted says.

I don't know, I say.

Twenty minutes, he says. Come for twenty minutes.

I don't know.

Doreeeen. Doreeeen Severrrrrna, he says in this weird low *Pet Sematary* voice.

You're such a baby, I say.

I'll buy you a cassingle if you come.

Whatever, I say, and I kind of laugh because me and Ted think "cassingle" is just about the stupidest word anyone's ever thought of.

I'll buy you a case of Tiger's Milk Bars, he says.

A case?

Well maybe not a case. Maybe like, five or something.

I go to Dad when the garage is done. He comes out to look at it with me because Jesus Christ knows he can't take my word for it. He scans the whole place like his eyes are searchlights going over the boxes and stacks and bags of things either he or Mom has to go through before I can throw them away.

What's all that? he says, pointing to three boxes in the corner, opened and ratty, with some papers spilling out.

They're Mom's, I say. They have her name on them.

Dad looks at me like I'm some kind of freak and says, And?

And, I say, and I thought she'd want to go through them herself.

I asked *you* to clean out the garage, he says, walking out. Not your mother . . . Just put aside whatever you don't know what to do with.

Then he leaves, and I'm alone again, burning up and bored as hell. I open the top box which says KATHY on it. I feel kind of bad for doing it. I get the feeling Mom doesn't know I'm going through her stuff. I mean, Dad's making me because he gets off on me being "productive" and shit. He probably didn't even think maybe Mom wants to go through her own stuff. Frankly, though, these boxes look so old, she could've forgotten they were even in here.

So aside from the huge asbestos cloud that comes out of the top box, there's a bunch of papers there. Some have my grandmother's name on them, and I figure it's like the will or the contract or something that she and Mom signed before Gram died.

Gram, Mom's mom, is the only grandparent I remember. All the rest died when I was little, but Gram lasted until I was ten. She was a nice old lady, but she was kind of scary. She had this cane she was always hitting everything with. She whacked Dad on the ass once with it, and I thought I was going to wet myself I was laughing so hard. She was laughing too, but she was laughing a little too *hard* for an adult, kind of. I was eight or whatever.

She would also get into singing these religious songs at the top of her lungs and totally off-key. She was all about religion. She would bang her cane along with the beat in her head whenever she damn well felt like it. Old people can do anything they want. She used to talk to pictures and birds and babies on the street. She called me Clara for awhile, and I never knew what the hell that was all about, but I didn't ask. I figured when she felt like calling me Doreen again, she would.

I kind of missed her when she died, because she always spiced up family get-togethers. Mom and Aunt Shirley would go back and forth about how crazy she was, and how shitty she treated them when they were kids, but I kind of enjoyed her singing and screaming and all that. It was something to look at, I guess.

I figure Mom probably wants to keep those papers because they're legal and everything, so I make a little "keep" pile and continue sorting. Then there's like, drawings that Tracey did when she was a kid, and a birthday card that I, apparently, gave to her when I was little. I figure she wants to keep those too.

Little pictures of Mom as a child, of her and Dad, of me and Tracey. Old papers, old things of Gram's. Letters to Mom and from Mom, to Dad and from Dad, labeled to Harry Severna. I pretty much figure she wants to keep all of it, because it's just the type of thing that would make her all emotional, even though it looks like none of this has been touched in years.

I have to lift the last box onto another, so I can sort through it without bending down the whole time and killing my back. But I guess I don't get enough of a hold on it because when I lift, the whole bottom falls out, and there are papers everywhere.

Shit.

I pick up the first thing I see, which is a postcard. It's a picture of all these buildings with CHICAGO, written across it in this cheesy pink cursive. I turn it over, and it's addressed to MOM & DAD SEVER-NA. Then I read the message:

Dear Mom & Dad,
FUCK YOU!!!
Love and kisses,
Henry

I almost start shaking.

I read it over about ten times, and each time I keep not believing it until I read it over the next time. It's postmarked from Chicago, Illinois, the year after he left.

I blow the dust off, thinking crazy for a second, like I'll blow off another layer, and there'll be a whole other letter from Henry there or something. But there's not.

It's obvious that Mom kept this for a reason and Dad probably doesn't know it's here. It sort of hits me that Henry's alive somewhere. I guess it's possible that he's not now, but I really think he is. I mean, I've always pretty much known that, but still, it doesn't really occur to me all the time. I'm too busy imagining him as some kind of ghost.

I start to wonder if Mom cried when she got this in the mail, or is it possible she laughed? I think it's a pretty funny postcard. She probably got it while Dad was at work. She probably hid it from him. I want to go up to her and shake it in her fucking face. I want to say, you're a fucking liar—Henry's not dead.

I think that's why people keep pictures and letters from people, especially if they're dead—because those things make them alive somewhere—in a little invisible bag floating around the air, not in any time in particular, but all the time. And forever.

I stand up and hold the postcard in my hands like it's a thousand dollars or something. I feel all charged up, like I've swallowed a six-pack of Jolt. I feel like running around the block. I feel like screaming. I realize that I'm shaking and I'm suddenly cold, and the sweat on me is making me colder. I think maybe I'm getting sick, coming down with something. I don't know what to do with myself—cry or throw up or start setting shit on fire.

I shove the postcard in my pocket and it feels all bulky.

Oh, I say out loud with my eyes closed, but it doesn't even feel like a real sound. Just breath with noise.

Then I feel my heart beat—I can feel it when I'm really quiet. And I leave the garage and squint my eyes because it's so bright—the sun reflecting off the white pavement—and I feel like I've been in there for about a week straight, and I figure that's what people who work in offices feel like when they leave in the afternoon.

For a second I think maybe there's more in that box, more from Henry. Something else, telling me something. I start to turn around to go back into the garage, but then Mom sticks her head out the door and yells that Ted's on the phone. So I go inside, and every time I step, I can feel Henry's postcard against my leg, scratching and pinching me almost. I reach into my pocket and ball it up even more, so that I can feel it no matter what I do.

What? I say as I pick up the phone.

Nice phone courtesy, Ted says.

Shut up, I'm hot and I'm busy, what do you want?

Fabulous mood, Dor.

Ted, I'm not happy right now.

So?

So stop messing with me. What do you want?

To lose my virginity.

Quit it, Ted—

Calm down, tiger, is it around that time of the month?

Not now . . . not now, I say, pacing around the living room, still shaking.

I get so angry at Ted sometimes, only when he's like this, though. He acts like it's his life's work to get on my nerves.

Have we not had our daily sedative? he says in this sugary doctor voice he has that usually cracks me up but now it's like anything he says is just going to make me more and more pissed off.

Ted, I'm hanging up, I say, closing my eyes, feeling thirsty and nervous and nauseous at the same time.

For some reason I can't tell Ted about the postcard just yet. It's like I need to have it in my pocket for a while. It has to sit there for a little while until I'm sure it's not going anywhere.

Oh, but why? Ted says, sounding like someone from a soap opera. Don't you love me anymore?

And then I pretty much lose it.

You can go to that goddamn party by yourself, *faggot!!!*

Then I slam the phone down so hard it rings a little when the receiver hits the base. I kick the table the phone's on and it shakes, and then I shut my eyes hard and try to breathe deep.

When I open my eyes, both Mom and Dad are standing in front of me, looking at me and not moving. Mom's holding a dishtowel and Dad's holding the newspaper and they're looking at me like I just got here from Jupiter. It's sort of funny, actually.

Then I get sent to my room for the second time in about three days for spazzing out, which doesn't bother me all that much because I've pissed off my only friend in the world anyway, so I'm probably not going to be needing to go out any time soon.

I lie very still on my bed and touch the postcard again, and I pull it out and read it, and I hold it against my chest, and I feel real emotional about it, like it's alive or something. I'm still cold and sweaty but I've calmed down a little bit, and I look up at the ceiling and try to picture Henry, dark and handsome, walking around Chicago on a sunny hot day, and I think maybe—maybe for this one second, for one stupid second, he's thinking about me. Just for the hell of it.

· · ·

I sit up in the bathtub, and I have a rich headache. The water's never high enough and it's always too hot. Sweat trickles down on my face even when I'm in the tub, and I taste it when it hits my lips. Salt.

I put the postcard on the toilet seat before I got in. I don't want it lying around. Even if I shoved it under my clothes or my bed, I'm still afraid something will happen to it. I think maybe Mom would find it or there would be a fire and I wouldn't be able to get to it.

I know it's a pretty stupid thing to do—I know there's not going to be a fire or anything—but I wouldn't be able to just sit in the tub or anywhere unless I could at least see the postcard. I feel real funny about it. I mean, I know it's not a person—I'm not nutty.

There's a knock on the door, and I jump a little and Dad says, Doreen, when you're finished in there, I need to speak with you.

I sigh.

Doreen? he says again.

Yeah, OK, I say. I'll be out in a second.

Sometimes I think Dad really talks strangely, the way he says things like "when you're finished in there." Finished with what? He makes it sound like I'm grouting the tub or something. At least he didn't ask if I was decent. I think that's kind of a dumb question because most people who close the bathroom door are naked in some way. Of course I'm glad he didn't just barge right in, and I'm doubly glad I'm in the tub instead of sitting on the toilet. That's just about the worst scenario I can think of. If somebody, *anybody,* saw me pooping, I just might have to die, or at the very least change my name and move to another country.

I step out of the tub and dry off quickly, pull my jeans and my T-shirt on, and I grab the postcard, which is all wrinkly now from being balled-up and steamed in the bathroom, and I shove it in my pocket.

Then I go into the living room where Dad is watching TV, and he mutes it and looks at me like he expects me to say something.

Sit down, Doreen, he says, and I sit on the edge of the couch, opposite him. For a second it's like we're going to have a normal conversation, like two human adults almost, but then he stands up and rubs his chin, and I know I'm in for it.

Your mother gets very disturbed by foul language, he says.

All of a sudden, I remember when I was little, and Mom was wiping my face clean, telling me she didn't want to hear the toilet talk. I spent a long time trying to figure out what the hell "the toilet talk" was until I realized it was dirty words. I don't know what I could've been saying at that age that was so bad. I was just a little kid—I can't imagine I was calling anyone a cocksucker just yet.

Yeah, I know, I say.

If you know, why did you scream those things? he says, getting all stern.

I just got angry at Ted, I say.

You're going to be angry at a lot of things in your life, he says.

Whenever Dad gets started on the "in your life" crap, it means he's really on a roll now.

You can't always throw a fit when someone makes you angry, he says, which I find a little funny, because Dad's had a few episodes when he's broken glasses because me and Tracey have left the living room messy or something.

You have to learn some self-control, he says. You can't let your temper get the better of you—you have to be stronger than that. Otherwise, you'll never make it anywhere.

I feel like saying, oh, OK Dad, I get it, if I say bad words I'm never going to amount to anything. It's really slick how he's making it seem like it's for my own good that I don't curse, like it'll be good for my career and indeed for the good of mankind as we know it, instead of just telling the truth, which is that Mom's a headcase and has heart palpitations when I swear.

Yeah, I know, I say.

You can't afford to be stupid like that, he says.

I nod and don't look at him.

That's all, he says quietly, and then he turns away and sits down and turns on the sound again.

I drag my feet back to my room and close the door and slide down and lean against it, and I think I couldn't get any more pathetic if I tried. I don't even want to think about the postcard in my pocket. I don't even want to think about what Henry would say. Standing in the corner, shaking his head at me. You pussy.

I figure maybe Ted's in the square because he goes there when he doesn't want to see me. It's pretty stupid of him, considering I *know* where he is when he's trying to avoid me. I know how to find him. The square's also a great place to skate, even though it's sort of been outlawed. But Ted's not that much of a skater to mind too much. He's a lot more into smoking than he's into skating. He doesn't dress like a skater either—he wears pants that basically fit. No one wears clothes that fucking fit anymore.

Ted's not exactly great at it either. He can get around and everything, but he can't do a bunch of tricks. The square is this tiny area behind this ice cream place. It's not real big, but there are a few concrete steps leading down from the back door of the store, and there's this weird old fountain or birdbath or whatever it is, which is all decrepid and falling apart. The skaters like the square because it's kind of hidden, and the people in the store can't hear any noise from the back, really. I hope the skaters aren't there today though, because I just see Ted in his small little way, taking a challenge from them. I can see him being all angry at me, trying to be all cool and wanting to let off steam and then falling on his ass.

The people in the ice cream place look at me weird. Lots of people look at anyone my age like they're stealing. I try not to look at them, and I walk around back, and Ted's there, and he's trying to get a lead off the fountain but he's not doing too well. He looks all tight, and his lips are all scrunched up.

Hey, I say.

He doesn't really look at me and keeps trying the fountain.

Hey, he says.

I'm sorry I called you a faggot, Ted, but I hate it when you get like that, I say.

He sort of laughs and doesn't look at me and keeps skating around the fountain.

It usually makes you laugh when I get like that, he says.

I just wasn't in a very laughing kind of mood.

Whatever, Doreen, he says.

Ted can just be such a whiner. I squat down on the pavement to sort of relax and let him know I'm not leaving. I know he doesn't want me to leave anyways.

My parents were really pissing me off and you called and you were being a real pain in the ass, actually, I say.

Well, fine, he says, still not looking at me but squinting over at the steps. But I was just kidding around—I didn't know how pissed off for real you were.

I want to say, But I *told* you I was, but I don't. I watch him skate around the square, all wobbly, trying so hard not to look at me, and it makes me feel a little ashamed. That's the thing about having one friend—you've got to be really careful about offending them.

Stop being angry at me, bitch! I scream across the square.

He looks at me out of the corner of his eye, and then he gets up on a few of the steps and tries to come down on his board, and of course he slips because *he can't skate for shit,* and he falls on his ass on the steps while the board coasts by me and hits the fountain. Then it rolls over like a dying animal, and the wheels turn in the air, and it sounds like a really quiet sewing machine.

I go over to him, and he sits up and curls over.

Ow ow ow, he keeps saying, leaning forward.

Are you okay? I ask.

No, he says, all pissed at me still and doubly pissed he fell.

Do you need some aspirin or something, I ask, like I carry a bottle around in my pocket.

No, I'm fine.

That's why nobody skates here anymore, you know, I say.

Everyone practically kills themself on those steps is the thing. I bet a thousand—

Just shut up, Doreen, Ted says.

I sit down next to him.

Why don't you try not being angry at me for a second, I say.

Ted exhales loudly.

I mean, I'm not going to that stupid party if *you're* not even talking to me.

Ted looks at me.

You want to go all of a sudden? he says.

For a little while, I say.

He smiles but I can tell he doesn't want to. Then we're just quiet.

I'm sorry I yelled, I say.

He shrugs and looks down.

Doesn't matter, he says. I figured you were in a bad mood or something.

Ted's such a dork. He throws this huge fit when I scream at him and then he tries to be all tough as if I've never met him before, and then he pretends he really understood and took the whole thing in stride. I look at him and he squints at his hand that he skinned when he fell, and I think about how Ted's not nearsighted or farsighted— he squints at everything. He just has shitty sight all across the board.

I put my hand on the side of his head and shove hard, and his head snaps to the side, and he smiles all crooked.

You dork, I say quietly, and Ted keeps smiling and gets a little red, like it's some kind of compliment.

Which I guess it sort of is.

• • •

When I get back, I tell Mom I'll probably be a little later than usual tonight. I can see her start to get all freaked out and paranoid because I'm sure she thinks me and Ted are going to get killed out on the dangerous streets of Pasadena.

Doreen, you and Ted go out late enough, she says.

What's this? Dad says as he comes into the kitchen with his empty glass.

Doreen wants a later curfew for tonight, Mom says with her eyes closed, as if she was telling him I wanted to go sell some heroin.

What for? Dad says to me.

There's this party, I say, and they both look at me. It's not going to be any big thing. . . .

Ted's throwing a party? Mom says.

No, not Ted.

Who's having the party? Dad says.

This girl from school—Alexandra Stuart.

Mom's eyes widen, and she starts to get all happy because she thinks this means I'm making friends with pretty girls.

Well, that should be fun, she says, beaming.

Where does she live? Dad says.

On Altamont.

Did you get an invitation in the mail? Mom asks.

No, I say.

Of course Mom would think I got an invitation in the mail. Yeah, Mom, she sent it to a printer. Your presence is cordially requested at 263 Altamont Avenue for cheap beer and fag jokes. Black tie.

Did she call you and ask you? Mom says.

No, me and Ted ran into her at Tower, I say.

And she asked you, just like that? Mom says, just absolutely entranced with all this. She's really into picturing how I got invited to what is in her mind the social event of the year.

Well, what a nice thing, she says. What a nice thing of her to do—she must be a very nice girl. . . . And Altamont is in a lovely neighborhood.

Yeah, Mom, she's the salt of the earth. That's the thing about Mom—I could tell her all the crappy things Alexandra Stuart does on a daily basis, and Mom would still think she's the ideal.

She's right about Altamont being in a nice neighborhood. I mean, the people who live there aren't millionaires or anything, but it's a little upscale. Mom's also got these screwy ideas about money. Sometimes I think that in her fantasyland, if someone has more money than us, then they probably deserve it and should have their asses kissed all the time. I think she kind of wishes we were all socialites, with like, balls and teas to go to and shit.

How much later than usual are you planning to be out? Dad says.

Probably an hour, hour and a half, I say.

Mom looks at Dad all hopeful because now she really wants me to go because she expects me to come back *transformed*—dressing like a girl and putting on makeup for three hours every morning.

No later than that, Dad says, and I can see Mom smile—this is a great big victory for her, apparently.

• • •

Before I go to Ted's, I head into the garage and I dig out the road atlas. It's big and blue and shiny and looks like it's never been cracked. When I open it, the binding snaps, and the pages are thin like money. It seems like a nice quality kind of book, and I think maybe Mom and Dad got it for a gift some time. For a second I wonder why they don't keep it in the house, and then I laugh, because they never *go* anywhere—why would they need a road atlas of the entire United States?

I start flipping through, and I see how the whole country's broken up into these tiny pieces, and each state is blown up to two or three pages. I find the page where Chicago is at the center, and I stare at the little black dot with all these red and blue lines running through it, like veins. There's like, a hundred little cities and towns around Chicago, and that kind of reminds me of LA, and I think maybe Henry lives in one of those little towns, and maybe it's a suburb like where I live. Where he used to live. But that's sort of nuts. I don't see why anyone would go to another place exactly like the one they came from.

I touch Chicago with my finger, the little black dot, and the page feels smooth. I close my eyes and tap it, try to picture it again, what it might be like there. I really don't know anything about Chicago. I don't think I've even seen a movie that takes place there. There's like, five thousand movies about New York and LA, but never anywhere in between, and there should be. Because people like, live there.

I flip through the atlas, and I think about how big it is, how so many people live in each state, each city, on each page, and it's a pretty overwhelming thing when I think about it. But at the same time it makes me feel close to everything. To Henry especially. It's like, yeah, it might be a big country, but someone can shove it all in a book that I can hold in my hands and look at on the floor of my garage.

I close the book and stare at it, press it to my chest. I shut my eyes and say out loud,

You there?

And I know no one's going to answer me, but if I close my eyes and get real quiet, I can picture Henry leaning over my shoulder, maybe his smoky breaths in my ear, and he says something very quiet, and I can't hear him at first. It's like we're separated by a window, but I start to see him clearer. Hands on my shoulders, scratchy voice, I can feel his body, warm behind me, hear him saying louder now,

Keep looking.

I drop the book and open my eyes, kind of dazed and dreamy. I look over at the stuff from the last box that fell on the floor, and I start going through it, slow for a second, through photos and papers, but then I lose my patience pretty quick, and I go through it faster and faster, but there's nothing. Nothing with Henry's name on it, nothing about him. I start to feel this stinging in my throat and eyes, like I'm going to throw up, but instead I scream. I scream and I thrash and I start ripping up everything I can get my hands on. I knock over boxes which I've stacked up. Fabrics fall in droopy piles and books hit the ground with hollow thuds. I rip apart papers that don't mean anything, with writing on them that I know is English but it might as well be Russian because I can't read any of it. Tears well up in my eyes and then I stop screaming for a second, and I realize that I better stop now because I haven't trashed the whole place yet, even though I'm pretty much going to have to start all over.

• • •

I go to Ted's as the sun is going down, and it's pretty funny—the sun setting wouldn't be half as pretty as it is if there wasn't any smog. It's all orange and smoky-looking, and the horizon's straight above the houses, like somebody took a ruler to it.

The screen door on Ted's house is flapping open and hitting the door frame, because for whatever reason, there's all these hot winds tonight. They don't really cool anything down when everything's so dry like it is, but maybe they'd feel nice right after you got out of a swimming pool or something. I start thinking about how maybe someone somewhere is getting out of a swimming pool right now, and I wish I was her.

Then I see that Ted's front door is a little open behind the screen door, which is a little more than weird. Ted always makes sure it's locked and everything because his mom isn't exactly big on details.

I open the screen door and push the front door open a little more, but I don't really go in.

Ted?

I don't hear an answer but I hear something in the kitchen—a chair move across the floor—and I get real freaked out for a second. But I figure it's probably Ted's mom and she probably didn't hear me—she always keeps asking me to speak up on the phone until I'm practically screaming.

I close the door behind me, and I walk through the entryway and take a left into the kitchen and I see Ted standing there, on the other side of the table, smoking a cigarette, looking down.

Why didn't you answer me? I say to him, and he turns to look at me and his eyes are all red.

Because I didn't fucking feel like it, he says, and he sniffles all loudly.

I think maybe he's been crying, and that's when I realize he's not just looking down for fun, but he's looking *at* something I can't see, so I walk around the table to stand next to him, and when I get there, I see.

It's his mom in her bathrobe, this blue flowery thing—everything she owns is flowery—and she's passed out, right there on the floor, and she looks a little dead almost, except she's breathing so heavy she sounds like a tractor.

Is she OK? I ask, because I really don't know what else to say.

She's fucking great, he says through his teeth. She hasn't done this in a really long time, he says, folding his arms and acting all fakely cheery. It's just really *cool* she picked tonight to pass fucking *out!!!* he screams, sort of right in her face, but Ted and I both know a live mariachi band wouldn't wake her up at this point.

Then Ted puts his hand over his face and he's breathing really hard and fast, and I think he might start crying, but I really hope he doesn't, for everyone involved. Sometimes crying really does make everything worse.

Ted, it's really OK, I say.

He takes his hand away from his face.

It's just . . . tonight, you know? he says quietly. She knew I was going out late tonight. She probably did it on purpose, he says, kneeling.

I'll help you carry her, I say.

We can't carry her, he says, all annoyed. Then he pulls her so she's sitting up a little and says, Her hair alone is too heavy for us.

A laugh slips out even though I don't mean for it to, but then I look at Ted, and he's sort of laughing too.

We should at least try, I say.

Ted looks down at his mom and thinks for a second.

OK, you get her feet, he says.

I grab Ted's mom's ankles, which are pretty fleshy, actually, and Ted laces his arms through her pits, and we both lift at the same time but Ted's mom's ass is just not going anywhere. She sort of looks like a hammock.

Come over here, Ted says, and I join him on the other side of her.

I look down at her face, at her smeared magenta lipstick and at her messy eyeliner. And all her dyed red hair all sloppy and teased on top of her head.

You take one arm, Ted says.

I take her right arm and Ted takes her left, and we start pulling and we're pretty successful. I mean, she's still a load, and it's harder to pull her once we get to the carpet in the hallway, but we get her to her bedroom somehow. The whole time there's this cigarette barely hanging from Ted's lip, and there's dead ash falling on the carpet and in his mom's hair, sort of—it makes us laugh in a weird kind of way. I mean, I know this is all pretty bad, and Ted must feel like real shit, but for whatever reason, dragging Ted's mom around by her arms is *really* funny at this particular second.

We get her to the bedroom, and after a few big heaves, we get her onto the bed. Her mouth is open, and her foundation has gotten on her hair a little bit. She's still making the tractor breathing/snoring noises, and she's sweating more than we are, it seems like.

Do we need to do anything else? I ask Ted, because I really have no idea what we're supposed to do next.

Not unless you wanna put her in her pj's, Ted says.

I shake my head because seeing Ted's mom naked is just not something I need to do. Not now. Not ever.

She'll be fine, Ted says, and he puts out his cigarette in the ashtray on his mom's nightstand.

Then we go back into the kitchen, and there are all these flies around because the front door was left open. I hate flies. They always get in my face, and any time one lands on me I just automatically think how it was probably sitting on top of a big pile of shit somewhere not too long ago.

You want a soda or something? Ted says.

We drink our sodas, and mine is really good. Tracey says you shouldn't drink sodas on hot days because it dehydrates you and that you should drink water. Soda's so good though sometimes, all bubbly and so sweet that your spit tastes sugary for the next hour or so.

Ted lights another cigarette, and I light one too, and I could start yammering about any stupid thing like the party tonight or Dad getting pissed because I swore or that band me and Ted are never going to have, but I don't, because sometimes, it's better not to talk just to hear yourself talking, and I know that. Ted's got to know it too, because he's not saying anything either. We're both just drinking our sodas and smoking and sweating, and only really moving to swat the flies away from our faces.

On the way to the party, me and Ted see this old guy trying to help this old lady, his wife, I guess, out of a car. There's a rickety old wheelchair all set up, which looks like it couldn't hold a pillow without falling apart, and the old guy, who's real old actually—he's got those big old guy ears hanging off of his head like wings and all sorts of spots on his face—he's trying to lift his wife out of the car. She's no small woman, and he's really too old to be hauling her around, but he lifts her. He wraps his arms around her, and she stands and holds onto the open car door and lets him lift her, and I can see where his hands are locked around her back, and her shirt rides up a little. His hands are all white, and she's holding onto him too. And then he plops her down in the chair, and it doesn't break or anything, which sort of surprises me. Then he shuts the car door, and he wipes his forehead with a Kleenex and he balls it up in his hands. And then he starts wheeling her up the driveway to their house, which looks all tinny and hollow. I look at their square front window, and it has those old-people curtains hanging in it—they look all long and thin and flowy and kind of see-through. I look away, though, when the light goes on inside, because I think I probably should.

And then there's the party.

Me and Ted don't talk much on the way there. We're both kind of inside our own heads tonight, I think because we both know it's so weird that we're going to this party. I'm a little nervous though for

some dumb reason, and I clench my fist real tight and feel in my
pocket for Henry's balled-up postcard.

It takes us a good forty-five minutes to walk there, because
Alexandra Stuart doesn't live in our neighborhood. I'm kind of glad
about it though, because we end up getting there around ten, and I
really didn't want to get there before anybody else.

Alexandra Stuart's house has a little pathway leading to the front
door, and there are some skaters sitting around on the steps of the
doorway.

Who is that? Ted says, squinting.

I shrug, and we walk up the pathway, and the skaters look at us
weird. I recognize them all from school but I don't know any of their
names, except Mark Mohr, who wears shorts every day and acts like
a reject from a Dr. Dre video.

He looks up at us and burps and then smiles. The skaters all laugh
like idiots then, and they all take swigs from their 40s. These guys
are all about *class*.

I don't look at Ted because I'm kind of afraid to. I'm afraid to see
him not have the time of his life, even though I knew this would be
hell from the very start. We step around the skaters as they start talking again. Everything's phat dope wack with them. I almost want to
turn around and kick them in the damn head and say I'm so sorry
I'm not as cool as you, that I don't wear clothes ten times my size
and have a supply of Olde English IVed into my veins at all times.

Ted opens the front door and we go in. The lights are dim, and
there's techno music playing with too much treble, and assholes from
school are everywhere. People are sitting in little circles, and there

are a couple of kids screwed up on ex or something, twirling around in the middle of the room. Goddamn hippies. They think just because they trip on the weekend and have sex with everyone that they're Janis Joplin or something.

And then the ravers. The scenester girls who look like mini Tracey's. Tight clothes and glitter on their faces, nail polish that looks like white-out.

I feel like I can't even move, like I'm suspended in the middle of this room, like me and Ted are on the other side of the glass wall, looking in at the freakshow, while they look at us and think we're the freakshow. And maybe we are.

You're either a pierced little kid–clothes raver or you're a hip hop blunt skater or you're an acidhead Jerry-tribute hippie or you're a english pop band mod or you're a whiny zine indie rocker or you're a rich kid junkie waiting to happen, or you're a cross between two or three, but I know I'm not any of them. And I thank God for it, because I'd rather be dead than be a zombie. If you pick one, you don't have to worry about who your friends are or what you do on the weekends, because it's already all set up for you. It's your basic choose-your-own-adventure lifestyle. Turn to page 52—You go to a stupid party and don't talk to anyone. Turn to page 64—You open the front door and drown in a tidal wave of bongwater.

You never live for very long in those books.

Oh, hey, the guy on ex says, looking at me and Ted like our faces are pinwheels. How are you guys, um, doing? he says.

The girl he's with is gripping onto his shoulder and laughing really hard. Every time she looks at me and Ted, she starts laughing.

I've seen them both around. That's the thing—I've seen everyone around—they've all seen each other around. Everyone's been around forever but nobody really knows anything about anyone else. But talking to these two, I don't know why you'd want to.

The girl whispers something in the guy's ear, and he starts to laugh. Then she kisses his neck and shoves a ring that's really a lollipop in his face, and he licks it and closes his eyes.

That's good, he says.

Then they start kissing, and I wince a little, and I look at Ted, trying not to be uncomfortable.

Come on, I say to him, and I pull him away from the lizards.

I hate tripping kids, I say to Ted. They're like fat people at a buffet—Try this, try this . . .

Me and Ted go into some bedroom, Alexandra's, I guess, and everything is done up in gray and black and white, and there are Christmas lights strung up all over the place. There's this lava lamp, which is the only main light really, but I think it's kind of broken because the stuff inside looks more like a baby alien than lava.

Some scenester kids are sitting on the edge of the bed, and they're passing a joint around, and they don't look at us when we come in.

Is this her room? Ted says to me.

I guess so, I say, and Ted goes off to look at her CDs, and I look at her dresser, which is so white and shiny and smooth it looks like it's made from tusks or something.

There are some pictures in frames on top—of her and her bitchy girlfriends, of her and Alex Matten the brainiac. I really want to open the drawers for some reason. It's not really a great habit to want to go through every damn thing that could be private to someone else. But then I think, What could Alexandra Stuart have that's so private? It's not like she's going to have a bunch of secret plans and blueprints lying around.

I look over at the scenesters, and they're all stoned and talking about rabbits.

I'm telling you, one girl is saying, I had this bunny for years . . . it was like a dog . . . we had, like, what the fuck—a leash for it.

Why didn't you just get a dog? some guy says, and then when the girl doesn't answer, the guy says, Your family is so fuckin' sketch.

I stop trying to hear what they're saying because I can only take so much intellectual conversation every hour, and the skaters on the front steps just plain tapped me out.

Instead I open the top drawer a little, and I see a bunch of lacy underwear and bras, and I see one that's velvet. I don't want to open it too much though, because I can just imagine the rumors that would be spread about me if I got caught going through Alexandra Stuart's underwear drawer.

I see this little white pillow that's making the whole drawer smell like baby powder, and I think about how much Mom would be into this. I can imagine her saying, Doreen, why don't you have a scented pillow in your underwear drawer? Because I'm not a *dork,* Mom.

I run my hand along the inside of the drawer, and I feel this little piece of paper, and I pull it out, and it's an envelope, an already-opened letter, with ALEXANDRA on the front in messy writing. A letter to Alexandra. I want to read it more than anything. I don't even know why. I don't really give a shit in a serious way about who's writing whatever to Princess Alexandra Stuart, but I just want to see what goes into her head for some reason.

Hey, Dor, Ted says, and I whip around real quick and paranoid, because I don't want him to know what I'm doing.

What? I say, holding the letter behind me, leaning against the drawer so it closes.

Let's go look around, he says.

Yeah, OK, I say, and I tuck the letter into my back pocket.

I don't even think about doing it, either. I don't think, Oh gosh, maybe I shouldn't or that's someone else's private property. I just don't care enough to care right now.

As we leave the room, one of the scenesters knocks his beer over, so that it gets on mine and Ted's shoes.

Sorry, he says all fakely, and they all laugh at us, and me and Ted don't say anything and just leave, because it's easier.

Hi, Doreen. Hi, Ted, Alexandra Stuart says, all sharp.

It seems like everyone in the kitchen turns to look at us. The gang's all here. Alex Matten, Karen Percy, Dave Campos, Josie Authwell, Peter Waitman. Alexandra's sitting on the counter, and everyone's huddled around. Dave is holding a bong, and some preppy kid in khakis, who looks way too old to be here, is packing it.

Hi, I say, and Ted sort of waves, and they all barely smile, and Alex Matten stares at Ted for a second and then turns to Peter Waitman again.

Then I'm sure they all go back to discussing the Bosnian crisis and scientific theories and shit. Ted and I are alone again, it seems like. We're just standing around in Alexandra Stuart's kitchen, watching them smoke a bowl. It's like a dream, kind of. Especially because there's a dim fluorescent light on above the sink, and it makes everyone look all yellow and gross.

Dave Campos takes a hit and blows the smoke out over Josie Authwell's head, right into our faces. I cough a little.

Sorry, Miss Severna, Dave says all snotty, and he hands the bong back to Mr. J. Crew.

Forget it, I say.

So, Ted, Dave says, leaving the crowd and coming up to us. You wanna do some shots?

Sure, Ted says without waiting a second, and I look at him.

He rolls his eyes at me like, don't be so stupid, Dor.

As soon as he says it, Alex Matten and Peter Waitman leave the crowd, and they go with Dave and Ted into the living room, and I do not have a good feeling about any of this. I remember going past these cows in a field once—we were on some kind of family vacation in Northern California, seeing all these sick-looking cows with tags on their ears. I sort of know what they were going through a little, I think.

Doreen, c'mere, Alexandra says, and I walk over to them.

She's wearing this cropped shirt so you can see her belly button, which has a ring through it, and her stomach's all perfect and flat and tanned, and she's got this gray pleated skirt on. I stare at her stomach and wish for a second that mine looked like that.

This is my cousin Brad, she says, pointing to J. Crew. He's from San Francisco.

I smile at J. Crew and he looks up for a second, but I am clearly not worthy of his attention. And my heart is breaking right in half because of it.

You know Josie and Karen, Alexandra says, and Josie and Karen say, Hi really quick like they'll turn back into pumpkins or maybe never get that dream date with the New Kids if they give up too much energy in saying hello to me.

Do you want a hit? Alexandra says, handing me the bong.

Maybe just one.

I really don't know how much time goes by.

I just know my head feels too heavy for my neck, and I want to lie down. Every time I think we're all done, J. Crew keeps packing and passing. Alexandra and Josie and Karen are yammering, and they're talking way too fast—it sounds like an African language or something—all clicks and short chopped words.

J. Crew doesn't talk to anyone, really. He just keeps packing, and he takes the first hit every time. He's really into smoking, I guess.

Doreen almost couldn't make it, Alexandra says to the other two, and there's something real sour about the way she says it.

Why not, Doreen? Josie says, almost laughing, and I'm sure she's thinking I couldn't possibly be *hip* enough to get in trouble with my parents.

I cough a little and say, I've just been staying out too late for the past couple of weeks.

Partying hard, are you? Karen Percy says, real sarcastic.

I picture me and Ted in his basement, smoking cigarettes and talking about our dumb band, and then I feel my face get red, and I'm kind of glad the yellowish light is on so they can't see.

I'll bet you are, Alexandra says, blowing rings of pot smoke into the air. I'll bet you and Ted just get crazy, she says.

I look down at my hands, which look all bony in the light, and I can hear them all laughing a little. I laugh a little too, for some dumb reason. As if we're in this together.

As J. Crew packs another bowl, and I have to lean against the counter for balance, Alexandra unwraps a pack of Parliaments.

Shit, she says, I fucking hate how there's so much loose tobacco in these.

And then she blows the loose tobacco chips in my direction, so that they get in my eyes. They really hurt too, and they make my eyes water and sting, and I reach into my pocket because I think maybe I slipped a Kleenex in there, but I didn't. But I do run my fingers along the creases of Henry's postcard.

So tell us, Doreen, Karen says, what *is* up with you and Ted?

Ted? I say, and my mouth is so dry I could die. I could really use a soda.

The three girls laugh like it's all some huge joke, and I feel like I need toothpicks to keep my eyelids from closing.

Yeah—Ted, she says.

He's pretty cute, Doreen, Josie says, real sarcastic. You two are really cute together.

I can feel my ears get all hot and a rock rise in my throat because

I'm embarrassed. They know it too. Whatever it is, whatever kind of gene they were born with that makes them want to pick at a person like they do is working at its max.

Are you guys fucking? Alexandra says to me, her eyes all stoned and evil.

All three of them look like jokers with wide smiles and pointy teeth. I half-expect them to pull out their pitchforks and start stabbing.

I look at them, and then I look at J. Crew, who seems to be nodding off and then he just leaves without saying anything and nobody seems to notice, and then I think about where Ted is, and then I think about how I wish Matthew were here, and then I think about how stupid they are and how stupid Tracey is, and then I think about how they'd laugh at me even more if they saw my slightly white-trashy aunt and uncle, and then I want to show them Henry's postcard like it's a bright hot light that will blind them for good. But I don't.

Are you? Alexandra says again, laughing.

All three of them—laughing.

Am I what? I say.

Are you and Ted, like, fucking? she says, and I can't stop staring at her mouth which never closes.

No, I say, and they all smile like they won something. And then I look straight at Alexandra and I say,

Are you, *like,* a mongoloid, or does your mouth just stay open like that because you're, *like,* a fucking idiot?

Then I figure it's probably time to go.

I stumble out of the kitchen, and I glance over my shoulder real quick to see the three of them looking kind of surprised, Josie and Karen saying something to each other, and Alexandra looking right at me, mouthing something but I can't tell what it is. I can't imagine it's good, anyway.

I go back into the living room, and I push past people and step over people, and some guy tugs hard on my jeans and says,

Watch where you're going, bitch.

Fuck you, pussy, I snap back to him, and as I keep stepping, I can hear him saying to his friends, What the fuck didshesaytome?

I know I really need to find Ted because I've had just about enough fun for one night, and at the rate I'm making friends, I figure I'm lucky if I make it out of here without getting my ass kicked. Or Ted's ass kicked, because most guys won't hit a girl.

I make a complete circle of the living room, and I still don't see Ted or any of the guys he left with, and then I see Dave Campos coming in from outside, holding a carton of cigarettes.

I go up to him and I say, Dave, where's Ted?

What? Dave says, putting his hand to his ear.

Where is Ted? I say louder.

I can't hear you, Madam Severna, the music's too loud, he says back, smiling.

The asshole can hear me. I know he can.

Where's Ted, goddamnit? I scream at him.

Suck my left one, sweetie, he says, sticking three cigarettes in his mouth.

You'd need *balls* for me to do that! I scream, and his face gets all tense.

I guess he heard me.

Fuck you! he shouts at me but I push past him and go out the front door and nearly trip over the skaters before he can say anything else.

They all kind of yell things at me but I can't really hear them because the music messed up my ears, and I'm still pretty stoned anyway. I step onto the front pathway, and I'm about to scream Ted's name I'm so desperate, when I see Alex Matten and Peter Waitman standing on the lawn, adjusting the sprinkler so that it soaks Ted to the bone, who's looking pretty unconscious, lying face down.

Oh shit, I say aloud, and I run toward them, and I trip over a rock on the pathway and sort of fall, and I hear the skaters laugh, and I hear Mark Mohr shout, Good job, slick.

I say, Fuck you, real quietly, and I'm sure no one hears but I don't care.

I get up off the ground, and now I have these green grass stains from the lawn all over my jeans, and I run to where Ted is.

I don't know, Doreen, Peter Waitman says, Ted here just drank too much.

What the fuck did you give him? I yell at them.

Hey, calm down, cool girl, Alex Matten says. It's not our fault your faggot friend can't hold his liquor.

I turn Ted over, and there's about four different shades of puke lying around his face. He's all wet too—soaked through his shirt, even his jeans.

You know what? says Alex Matten. You better get him outta here. Alex is going to be pissed as hell if the cops show up because some neighbor calls in that there's a drunk on the lawn.

Yeah, says Peter Waitman. Clean this shit up.

Fuck you, fuck you, I keep saying, but I don't look up at them. I can't.

I can't do anything because this is the closest to dead I've ever seen anyone. He looks so skinny and sick. I almost want to cry because I hate everyone so much all the time and because I want to shout at them, to tell them what kind of a night Ted's had—to tell them how bad everything is for him, for us. But they wouldn't care anyway. They don't care about anything.

I try to wake Ted up, and he opens his eyes a little but doesn't say anything—he just looks at me all confused, like I'm someone he knew in preschool or something.

Ted, come on, I say, and I pull him up, and he sort of stands but he's leaning against me hard.

His breath smells like throw-up too, which is really a great thing, and his arm is slung around me. I try to get him to walk off the lawn, and the sprinklers are still on and not making anything better, and pretty soon I'm soaking wet too, and this whole situation is making me feel real sober real quick.

Come on, Ted, I say.

What? Ted says, real vague, like he's at the other end of a tunnel or something.

We've got to walk, I say, but not really to him, more to me.

Ted doesn't do so great with the walking. It must be a real hassle teaching babies to walk, but it might be a little easier, because most babies don't throw back the Southern Comfort like there's no tomorrow.

Ted's not such a big guy, but he's too big for me to practically carry. I mean, I'm not so weak a girl, but I'm not a goddamn American Gladiator. I could probably pull off carrying an average-sized dog around, but not another person.

We get halfway down the block so that no one from the party can hear us really. Actually, I just assume they can't hear us because we can't hear them.

Then I just kind of let Ted slouch a little, against some bushes, and I almost start crying because I can't *carry* him anywhere, and I know I have to get him home, and *I* have to fucking get home, and I'm all wet and I smell like puke now, and so does Ted.

I wish there was someone I could call, someone who drove. I couldn't call Tracey, not in a million years—I'd never hear the end of that one, and she's probably not even home anyway. I would almost call Matthew, but I don't have his number. I don't even know his number. I don't have any money to get a damn cab. I start thinking how maybe I could get a cab somehow and then go to Ted's and leave Ted in the cab while I'd go in and go through his mom's purse to find some money. But there's no guarantee there'd be anything there, seeing that she was saucing up at bars all afternoon.

I start having a fantasy that maybe Matthew will drive by, just by chance, or maybe because he somehow knows I'm in trouble.

I'm such a fucking idiot.

Henry. Henry, please drive up. I can picture him almost, driving up in some beat-up car, wearing sunglasses. He kicks the shotgun door open. Come on kid, he says. Maybe somehow.

No way. No Matthew, no Henry. No fucking way. I am so fucking fucked it is not to be believed. I sit down on the pavement, with Ted's barfy body leaning up against me, his eyes rolling back into his head sort of. It's kind of freaky and I'm glad I can feel him breathing.

I seriously consider praying or something, but I can't for the life of me think of the second sentence of the Our Father, which isn't surprising, seeing that I've only been in a church, like twice ever.

So I get up, and I drag Ted a couple of feet, but I know that's not going to work either, and I hear music real clear all of a sudden—it's too loud to be coming from the party. It's this old Pavement song. Summer babe. Summer baby. Whatever.

I look around, and I figure it's probably not coming from the shrubbery so I look at the cars parked along the curb and figure it must be coming from someone's tape deck inside.

Come on kid, I think to myself, and I get a chill all over.

Then I walk a few feet to the corner, and next to me is this big boat of a Mercedes—one of those that takes up entire streets, and there's someone leaning back in the driver's seat, and when I get closer, I see that it's J. Crew. His head's back and his eyes are closed, and he's smoking a cigarette.

I knock on the window and his head jolts up, and he looks at me, all confused, and he seems all drunk and stoned, and he stares at me hard, and I don't think he recognizes me too well from the party.

I knock again, and he presses some button, and the passenger-side window buzzes down, and I lean in a little.

Hi, I say.

He doesn't say anything. He just still looks confused.

Look, I say, I know I don't know you at all—

He holds his hand up for a second, and I stop, and then he leans forward and turns the music off. Then he looks back at me.

I know I don't know you, I say again, but I was just at your cousin's party.

He's still looking at me like he has no idea what I'm talking about. I might as well be communicating by smoke signal.

Your cousin . . . Alexandra, I say, and still, he doesn't show any sign that he is understanding. So I just keep going and I point to Ted and say, I have no way to get home, and my friend's really sick, and I can't carry him.

I say it all real quick, and J. Crew looks over his shoulder at Ted, who's this wet barfy heap on the sidewalk, and I get a little discouraged. I mean, *I* probably wouldn't give us a ride anywhere.

J. Crew doesn't say anything at first, and then he leans over and opens the passenger door for me, and I see that he has a bottle of some kind of liquor between his legs, and it worries me a little, but it's not like I can afford to be picky at this point.

Get your friend, J. Crew says real quietly, without looking at me, and I'm so relieved I could scream.

But I don't. I run over to Ted and I pull him the few feet, and he's kind of awake, but only in a sleepwalky kind of way, I think, because he's mumbling something but I can't make it out. I'm not really trying that hard to either. I open the door to the backseat of the Mercedes, and I lift Ted up as much as I can.

Ted, move your damn ass, I say to him.

Then Ted looks up at me and smiles and says, You try to molest me in the parkin' lot.

I laugh in his face and almost want to give him a big hug or something stupid like that, but instead I pull him up a little, and he manages to scoot up enough so that his ass is on the backseat, and then I lift his legs, and shove him in, and he lies down and makes these squeaky noises, shifting around on the leather like he is. Then I slam the door, and it sounds like a safe, and I move to sit shotgun, still laughing a little, thinking some part of Ted's brain is still working, the part that controls his ass and remembers Pixies lyrics apparently.

I slip into the passenger seat, and I pull the door shut, and it makes the same heavy safe sound, like we're in a submarine. J. Crew takes a sip from whatever he's drinking—it looks like whiskey, I think, and he closes his eyes for a second and then looks at me.

Your friend better not puke in my mother's car, he says.

Oh no, he won't, I say, even though Ted's making these nasty gurgling noises.

There's one other condition, J. Crew says.

If he makes me do some weird sex thing, I don't know what I'll do.

What? I say quietly, staring straight ahead, not even looking at him a little just in case he starts beating off or something sick like that.

He taps my shoulder, and I look at him sort of sideways. He reaches his hand out, and there's a ring of keys dangling from his finger.

You drive, he says.

Hey, I can't drive, I say, almost laughing.

Sure you can, J. Crew says slowly. This is America. You can do anything.

No, the thing is that I don't have a license.

This is easy. This isn't even a stick—it's an automatic, he says.

Look, I say to him because I figure I better take this slow, since he doesn't seem to be getting it too well. I say, I don't have a license to drive a stick or an automatic. I don't have a license to drive *anything*.

Don't worry. It's easy, J. Crew says.

I can't do it, I say to him.

Alright, he says, taking his keys back. Looks like you don't have a ride then.

He leans his head back on the seat again, and I turn around and look at Ted, who's all spread out like a pressed flower, and I look back at J. Crew, who takes another sip of his whiskey.

OK, I say to him.

J. Crew doesn't do anything, and I'm about to say it again, when he sits up and opens the door and gets out of the car, and I watch him walk around the front and spit on the sidewalk and come around to my side. I move over into the driver's seat, and I put my hands on the wheel, which is huge and cold.

J. Crew slips into shotgun and slams the door and looks over at me.

Any time you're ready, he says.

I nod and stare at the dashboard, which is huge and high. I put my feet on the pedals just to feel them, and I have to stretch to feel them at all.

Here, J. Crew says, and he presses another button on the island between us, and my seat moves forward.

I hold the wheel a little tighter now, and I figure I better put on a seat belt, seeing that I've never driven before, and I'm probably going to *kill myself*. I sort of wish I had put a seat belt on Ted, but I really don't want to try to make him sit up, because that might make him throw up some more. J. Crew doesn't seem too concerned about any of this.

Start the car, he says, handing me the keys, holding the one up.

I nod, and I put the key into the ignition, and I turn it, and the engine starts up like a chainsaw that I can feel under my feet and my ass. The Pavement song blasts back on too, and it's a little shocking.

J. Crew reaches forward and turns the tape off so there's silence again.

Put the hand brake in, he says.

What?

The hand brake next to you. Push the button on the end and push it down.

OK, OK, I say, more to myself than to him, really.

Something about this whole night. I've felt like I was by myself the whole time.

Put the car into drive, he says.

Drive, I'm thinking. OK, drive. I look around by the hand brake and get real confused for a second.

It's the one with the *D* next to it, he says, all annoyed, and I kind of want to say, Hey, sorry I don't know what the *hell* I'm doing but this was your stupid idea.

I know, I know, I say to him.

Put the headlights on, he says.

I start to look around the wheel again, and then he leans over and clicks them on.

Thanks, I say, and I still feel like I'm about a foot tall compared to this huge car.

Right's gas, left's brake.

Yeah, I know, I say, and I look behind me.

I'm kind of glad I live here for once because there aren't a bunch of cars racing around at this time of night. It's not exactly a booming metropolis.

What are you waiting for? he says all angry.

I've just, I've never done this before. Just give me a second, I say to him.

I look ahead at the street, and it looks wide and gray, and I just keep thinking, fifteen minutes from now, I'll be at Ted's, and everything will be fine. OK. OK.

I tip my foot on the gas, and the car jerks forward and then I press a little lighter.

Turn the wheel, J. Crew says.

Yeah, I say, and I turn it a little, and the car starts to lurch forward some more, and I get it out onto the street, and we actually start moving down Altamont. As freaked out as I am, it's kind of a cool feeling—different than riding, it feels like I'm floating around, kind of.

You know my cousin, J. Crew says to me.

Um, yeah, I say, trying to pay attention to what the hell I'm doing.

Are you a friend of hers? he asks.

I don't really know how to answer him. I mean, I can't tell the truth—that she's a real bitch and that I just called her a mongoloid—but I probably couldn't get away with saying I'm her best friend. Yeah, me and her are tight, that's why I'm dragging my friend here down the sidewalk *away* from the party, asking strangers for rides.

Sort of, I say.

She's a fucking pricktease, J. Crew says, and he spits out the window, and I don't even want to know why Alexandra's *cousin* thinks she's a pricktease. I don't want to know what kind of weird stuff goes on in someone's family.

Oh, uh, really? I say, and then I realize I have to make a turn at the next intersection.

Yes, really, J. Crew says.

I have to turn, I say, and I'm a little scared about it.

So turn, he says.

Should I signal or something?

You don't have to signal when there's no one around, he says.

I'm beginning to think J. Crew should write his own California Driver's Handbook, seeing that he seems to be making up new rules every time he feels like it.

Now I'm going down the middle of the damn street, because I don't want to get near the parked cars on the sides. I look in the rearview mirror, and there's nothing but more gray street.

Then J. Crew starts laughing. I glance at him, and he's looking down, laughing to himself. He's really cracking himself up.

Did you have fun at that party? he says.

Yeah, it was a blast, I say all sarcastic, because I figure if he skipped out early, he probably wasn't having too much fun either.

Then we come to another intersection, and there's another car at the stop sign, crossing my path.

Oh shit, I say.

Just let him go first, J. Crew says, and I do, and then I take my foot off the brake and start going again.

Go faster, he says.

Hey, I don't know what I'm doing, I say.

There's no one around—you can go faster.

This speed is fine, I say, and I look at the speedometer and see that I'm going twenty.

Go faster, or you have to get out right now, he says, more pissed off.

I'm just about to call it a night and say Fine, pal, you can shove your stupid ride right up your asshole, but then I think about Ted, and I think maybe J. Crew's right. So I press the gas a little more.

Keep going, J. Crew says.

So I press a little more and a little more, and I guess this car's kind of old because it starts rattling a little, but I press a little more anyway, and the streetlights and the houses are going by in blurry flashes, and the street keeps curling up in front of us, and we're really sailing now, and suddenly I'm not scared too much anymore but I have this real excited feeling, like the car could really take off in the air if I go fast enough. I'm holding the wheel tight, and I'm not looking in any mirrors, which I can't imagine is a great idea, but I feel like J. Crew's running the show right now. I almost feel like he wouldn't let anything bad happen. Which I guess is pretty stupid seeing that he's just some drunk kid.

I have to turn, I say.

Slow down a little, J. Crew says. Brake a little.

I do, and the car screeches a little as I turn. I'm sliding all over the big leather seat, and in the middle of the turn, I hear Ted fall like a sack of bricks onto the floor in the backseat. The car turns like it's a train on tracks—more like Thunder Mountain at Disneyland actually, and when I straighten back out, I start speeding again.

I feel like laughing, and I start thinking about how I can't wait to get my license and listen to the Pixies in the car. It's like I've sucked helium out of a balloon the way I feel all floaty and weird. J. Crew looks relaxed like he just goes around making junior high kids give him rides all the time. Although what do I know—maybe he does. Maybe that's his life up in San Francisco. You never know up there.

Then I get to Ted's street, and I slow up a little, and I take my foot off the gas and just coast, and I hold the wheel steady. Then I brake real hard in front of Ted's house, and me and J. Crew jerk forward, but Ted can't really get any more on the floor so I don't feel too bad.

Put the brake in, J. Crew says, and I do, and then he tells me to put the car in neutral, so I do, and then I'm left with nothing to say.

Thanks for the ride, I say, because I don't know what else to do.

J. Crew nods and I figure he's waiting for me to leave, so I get out, and I open the door to the backseat and I poke Ted a few times, who's faceplanted back there.

He groans a little and says, What? all annoyed, like I'm being so unreasonable for wanting to get him into his house.

Ted, you've got to walk a little, I say.

I can sleep here, he says, his face all smushed against the side of the seat.

No you can't, I say. Come on.

Then I try to lift him, and he starts to move a little. He stumbles out of the car, and I'm holding him up with both arms, still, but at least he's sort of standing. I kick the door closed, and then I watch J. Crew move over into the driver's seat. He takes a big sip of whiskey, draining the bottle, and then he waves, all fakely cute.

The Pavement song comes back on, and he peels off like nobody's business, and I see him throw the whiskey bottle out down the street, and it smashes into a million pieces, and I watch the Mercedes swerve off and screech on the turn at the corner, and then I'm alone again, holding Ted up, and for the rest of the night, I keep wondering if it all really happened. I mean, I *know* it did—I'm not going batty—but I sort of have to remind myself that I didn't just make up J. Crew and his mother's Mercedes and the Pavement song. And I really wish Ted was awake and himself enough to talk about it. He probably won't remember anything. I wish I could be happy that it's my own private thing, that I drove and everything, but I do kind of wish Ted was awake, because then he could always remind me how cool it was.

I slip the key into my front door, and the house is pretty quiet and dark. I don't think I'm too late, especially since we weren't at the party all that long.

I take off my shoes in the living room so I make the least amount of noise possible, and then Dad comes out of the kitchen in his bathrobe, and he looks all weird to me—all tensed up and too much to drink.

Doreen, it's late, he says.

I look at the clock on the wall real quick and then I say, I'm not any later than I said I would be.

I'm not prepared to argue with you, Dad says, closing his eyes. You're fourteen years old, and it's too late for you to be coming home.

I want to tell him the kind of night I've had. I also want to tell him again that I'm really pretty on time, and that he OK'd me being out this late and everything, but when Dad's in this mood, when he's "not prepared to argue," it means he's not prepared to be wrong.

OK, Dad, I say. I'm sorry.

Then I turn around to go to my room, and he grabs my wrist tight so I can't move.

Don't do it again, he whispers, holding one finger up in my face.

I nod, and he drops my wrist, and I walk real quick into my room, and I close the door behind me. Then I stand on the other side of the door real quiet for a few seconds, and I hear him walk down the hall, and I hold my wrist, which is a little red, and then I hear his door open and close.

My heart's beating deep, and I pull Henry's postcard out of my pocket and feel it between my fingers for a second, and I shove it in my underwear drawer. Then I take off my jeans and my socks and my bra, and I climb into bed, and I'm suddenly not so exhausted anymore, which is weird, but my head's all jammed up with everything that happened tonight. I start to get real angry when I think about what those assholes made Ted drink. They probably told him he'd be a pussy or something if he didn't drink everything real fast. Boys are so fucking stupid.

Then I hear footsteps coming down the hall again, and I close my eyes just as a reflex, because I'm thinking if it's Dad and he peeks in, I want him to think I'm asleep. Then there's a light knock on my door, and I just lie there like a sock and don't do anything. Whenever people pretend they're sleeping, though, in a movie or something, it always looks so fake.

I hear the door open and close quietly, and then footsteps in my room, and my eyes are still closed, but I probably look real unnatural, the way I'm breathing and everything. I can feel sweat on my back, and I really wish I could kick the covers off me, but I don't want Dad to know I'm awake, and I wonder what the hell he's doing anyway.

Doreen, wake up.

I open my eyes, and it's Matthew standing there, and I jump a little because he sort of takes me by surprise, and I sit up.

Hi, I say.

Hi, he says, and his eyes look huge and wild, and he looks gigantic to me, standing up straight like a tower or something.

It's OK, he says, You can lie back down.

I think it's kind of strange he tells me to lie back down, but I do anyway, and I feel naked without a bra on, and I still want to kick the covers off me, but I can't with him standing there.

Then he lies down next to me, on top of the covers, and everything's so quiet, my mattress squeaks a little, and I feel his leg against mine, and my mouth gets real dry.

How was your night? he says.

It was OK, I say.

Just OK?

Well . . . yeah.

What did you do?

I went to this party.

How was that? he asks, turning his head, and he's so close I can smell his breath, which is smoky. I don't look at his eyes though. I can't.

Stupid, I say.

Parties usually are, he says.

I want to tell him about the whole night, about me calling Alexandra a mongoloid and everyone laughing at us and the stupid skaters and Ted's mom and Ted puking and J. Crew and me driving home. I feel like he'll know what I'm talking about.

Do you like me, Doreen?

Sure, I say.

You can't say "sure." Either yes or no, he says.

Yes.

I like you too.

Do you like Tracey? I say.

Tracey's a nice girl, he says.

A nice girl? He talks to me like I'm thirty or something.

Then he cups his hand on my chin and turns my head to face him, and I think I don't know what to do. I can feel myself sweating, and he puts his face up against mine so he can whisper something in my ear, and I can feel his warm cheek and I can't think of anything—my mind's really blank—empty space—I picture it like a newspaper without the print, and I feel like I'm across the room, watching all this happen, and all I can feel is his hand on my chin and his face next to mine.

But I think I like you more, he says.

Then he moves to lie on his side and his shirt hikes up a little. I can sort of see the sun tattoo. Black pointy rays and its round center. I almost don't want to move, like if I do, everything'll break like glass.

Do you like my sun? he says.

I guess, I say quietly.

Do you want to touch it? he says.

I don't know what to say. I don't know what to do. I don't know anything. I look up at him, at his black eyes and his lips, and I have to remind myself to breathe.

Here, he says, and he reaches for my hand, and I let him take it.

I just let my hand go limp in his, and his hand's all warm and huge and a little rough-feeling, and then he pulls my hand slowly to his stomach and lays it flat on top of the sun. His stomach is smooth and warm too, and the sun doesn't feel any different than the rest of his stomach, which sort of surprises me. I've never touched a tattoo before, so what do I know.

He closes his eyes like it feels really good to him, and I just don't want to move because I don't want to do anything wrong right now.

I like you so much, Doreen, he says. You're so perfect, he says.

I feel my face get all hot. Maybe people who get boyfriends all the time are used to this kind of thing, but I'm not.

Then he opens his eyes and whispers, Come here, and he puts his hand on the back of my neck and pulls me to him.

And then he's kissing me inside my mouth, his tongue moving all slow—I can feel it against my teeth, and it's sort of shocking. I'm not breathing at all, and I don't want to move because his hands are on my face, his fingers brushing down my cheeks, in my hair. It feels like my stomach's dropping out, like wind is blowing through me, and I feel myself get wet and I get embarrassed because of it and don't want him to know.

Then he stops and pulls away from me and is just holding my head there, and his hand is tight on my neck and he's staring at me, and then he lifts his other hand to my mouth and covers it.

Shhh, he says.

Then he gets up and he's gone, and I don't even hear the front door close, and I put my head on the sheets where he was lying, and I look for his smell but all I can smell is the sweat on me. Then I twist and turn, and I'm too hot and I'm too cold and it's just no use trying sleep anyways, and I'm too hysterical inside and I'm too scared, and I think I see the lights of a UFO coming through my window at some point and then I convince myself there's a ghost in the room, and then I wonder how people go around getting kissed all the time like it's not a big deal—Tracey and Alexandra Stuart and Alex Matten and everyone. I can't even think like a normal person, but maybe it's not always like that but really I don't care who you are or what you do, after something like that, you can't just get up and go through your day without everything being different, and then I fall asleep just as the first shots of sun come into my room and onto my wall like a spotlight.

PART TWO

When I see Ted, he looks like a goddamn cancer patient, all skinny and sick and like somebody just unhooked him from a respirator. We're in the basement, because his mom's been unloading the dishwasher for like, an hour and a half. Ted's drinking a Sprite really slow and smoking.

I puked in the shower this morning, he tells me.

How much did you drink for chrissake?

I don't know. I don't know, he says, rubbing his eyes.

They just told me to keep drinking.

Were they drinking?

Yeah, he says. They matched me shot for shot.

I can just picture Alex Matten and Peter Waitman and Suck My Left One telling Ted he was a queer if he didn't drink a liter of 90-proof.

Well, they must've been drinking iced tea or something, because they didn't look too hammered when they left you on the lawn, I say, suddenly all pissed.

Shit, I didn't know, Ted whines. They just kept pouring shots. What the fuck was I *supposed* to do?

Maybe not drink, I say.

But I know how it was. Staring in the face of those kids, them acting all nicey comfy like Ted was their best fucking friend.

Maybe they didn't know I'd get so drunk, Ted says quietly.

Don't you fucking get it? I say, standing up. They invited us to that party so they could make you puke and get me stoned and laugh at us like always.

Don't get angry at me, Dor, Ted says, all pathetic. But I already am. Sometimes I hate thinking about Ted and all the times we laugh so hard our faces hurt and we have to pee, and all the times we tell each other dumb shit because we know the other will listen. Sometimes I hate thinking about all that because when I think about the way everyone else in the whole damn world looks at us, that other stuff just gets all ruined. It all just gets shot to shit.

You should have known, I say, maybe a little too loud.

Excuse me, Ted says. Excuse me for not being as *smart* as you, he says, all defeated, and then I'm sort of sorry.

I sit down next to him again, and I take one of his cigarettes and light it.

That's not what I mean, I say.

What *do* you mean?

That— I say, but I don't finish because I don't know what I mean.

What does a person do in this fucking life, is what I mean, but I don't say that to Ted. What does a person do? You just open your mouth and kneel down and let people piss and shit all over you. You just let them do anything. You just sit there and let them take clean shots at you until you're all broke.

I don't know, I say.

I look at Ted and I am angry at him. Because he's so little and weak and believes whatever people say and because he's stupid enough to be my friend.

I go home, because me and Ted don't seem to have much to talk about, which is kind of weird since so much happened last night. I told him I drove and everything, and he was a little interested, but I think he's just mostly hungover and sick. And a little sad, because I made him feel bad. I don't know why I got so angry at him. It's not his fault Alex Matten's an asshole.

I didn't tell him about Matthew, even though when I looked in the mirror this morning, I touched my face and lips and teeth and I thought about him. I have been all day. And I get that inside chill again and feel sick to my stomach a little every time.

I get home and it's quiet, and I figure Mom went out to run errands, and Tracey's not around, and Dad's at work. Though it's kind of nice to be alone. And since there's no one else to talk to, I think about Matthew some more.

I get a soda from the kitchen and then I go into my room, and I open the window even though the air conditioning's on full blast. Then I look at my bed, which Mom made, I guess, and I get kind of pissed because I kind of wanted to lie in bed for a while and just think.

I know it's stupid. I know Matthew wouldn't appear or anything, but I still wanted to lie around in the place where he was, where we were.

I go into the bathroom to pee, and when I'm done I put the soda on the sink, and I look at myself in the mirror. I go up to it and put my face against it so I steam it up. Then I step back and look at me up and down, and then I take off my shirt.

You can have it, I say to myself, and I hold the shirt out to the mirror.

Then I look at my breasts, and I hold them for a second, and then I let my hands slide down sort of to my stomach. Then I stop and look at myself from the side, and I pull my hair back and I run my fingers along my face. Then I take off my jeans and I put my hands on my thighs, and I'm standing in front of the mirror the whole time, and my skin feels smooth to me, and tight, but I don't know if I think that because it's mine and I'm used to it and I don't have pockmarks and goiters and shit, or because it really is smooth. Tracey has like, a hundred different kinds of lotions, and I guess her skin is pretty smooth, but I don't put anything on my skin, and I think it's OK. I think it would be OK for someone to touch.

I sit down on the tile, and I'm in my underwear and bra still, and the tile's cool and it feels nice. Then I hold my bare feet, and I have these nasty yellow calluses that I've had all my life. I never used to wear shoes when I was a little kid, apparently. Aunt Shirley told me once that I used to tell strangers that my parents were too poor to buy me shoes and that's why I was running around barefoot. I'm sure Dad wasn't really into that, me making everyone think he was some kind of louse.

Then I look at myself in the mirror again, and I bite my bottom lip, and I rub my eyes and I know I'm all red-eyed and I've made my lip kind of swollen, and I open my mouth and look at my teeth again, and I run my tongue over them with my eyes closed, and then I hear the front door open and Mom's voice, and I get up and put my clothes on real quick, and I take my soda so no one will know I've been in here.

Mom asks me something I don't hear.

What? I say.

How was the party? she says, all beamy, putting bags of groceries on the counter.

You went to a party? Tracey says, all disbelieving, pulling apple juice out of a bag.

It was fine, I say.

Whose party? Tracey says, almost laughing at me.

Alexandra Stuart's, I say.

Mom takes a big box of detergent and a thing of bleach and leaves the kitchen.

Did you drink? Tracey says, all interested—sort of, like she thinks I'm lying and she's trying to trip me up on it.

No.

Why not?

I didn't feel like it, I say.

Did you smoke up? she says.

No.

Why not?

Tracey looks like a little rat when she asks questions—her nose gets all scrunched. She's pretty little anyway. I'm already taller than her. I hate girls who are all little and cute and shake their tiny little asses around.

Why didn't you smoke up, Dor? Tracey says.

I didn't fucking feel like it, I say.

Tracey's face unscrunches, and her eyes get narrow and her mouth gets all tight.

What's up with all the hostility, Dor? she says.

When I don't answer, she says to me, You're so fucking dumb, and then she leaves.

And I should call after her, If I'm so fucking dumb, then why is your damn boyfriend smooching me? Instead I just stand there and smile for no good reason like an idiot.

• • •

I end up watching TV because there's nothing else to do really. I could go and clean out the garage again, but that doesn't really sound like too much fun to me.

I'm not even really watching anything. I just keep flipping channels, and there seem to be commercials on every station. Whoever thinks up ideas for commercials must be so fucking stupid. They must just sit around and eat donuts and think of stupid things that other stupid people will laugh at.

For some reason, whoever's in charge thinks that anything to do with twins is hilarious. They must really get their rocks off when twins are involved in any way, like: Twin A rides a bicycle past a fruit stand, and then Twin B rides by, and the fruit stand guy scratches his head and just can't get over it. I'm so sure grown adult twins walk around wearing matching outfits so they can confuse the old guy down at the fruit stand. If *I* ever saw adult identical twins wearing the same clothes, I'd probably run in the other direction. I'd probably think they had a chemical imbalance.

I bet these guys take it real seriously too. Especially when they're thinking up the commercials for like the Superbowl and the Grammys and stuff. The Superbowl must be the event of the year for the commercial people. I remember Dad and Uncle Bill watching the Superbowl last year, laughing like idiots at all the beer and car commercials. And then Mom came in and giggled like she just got asked to the prom or something, and she said something dumb like, What cute frogs. Then I just must've left the room because I couldn't handle it. It really pisses me off when people pay attention to stupid shit.

So I stop flipping at this one commercial, and all these surfer type tools are running around the beach, and all these girls in bathing suits are running around with them, and they're all being really cute, splashing water in each other's faces and playing volleyball and carrying each other around on piggyback, and these huge words flash on the screen: THIS IS HOW WE *DO* SUMMER IN CALIFORNIA . . . ANY QUESTIONS? Then the last thing they show is this girl getting dumped in the water by all her really good friends, and everyone's laughing like it's so incredibly funny, and they show the girl's face and she's laughing so hard it looks like her face is going to crack open, and she's looking at all her friends like, Oh you *crazy* kids. That's exactly why I love you guys—you're always dumping me in the ice-cold Pacific. I think that's the thing I hate—how much of a fucking lie everything is. I've lived in California my whole life, and I've never seen anyone like that on the beach. The only surfers I see are all stoners and so drugged-up they're all thin and pale, and when the sun goes down they all play their guitars until they pass out.

It's not like I hang out at the beach too much either. The only beaches I've been to are all cruddy, and there's broken glass and needles everywhere. You could catch a disease just taking a walk.

Point is, I don't know who *does* summer like that. No one I know does anyway. And they probably made that commercial for people in other states, so that they'd all want to come here. That's what I hate, though, about commercials and lots of other things too—they all seem to be made for someone else.

I'm lying on my bed, listening to music, when Mom comes in with clean folded clothes. She goes right to the stereo and turns it down, and I hate it when she does that because I put it on that loud for a reason, and it also means she's probably going to say something.

That's just on way too loud, Doreen, she says as she starts putting my shirts and underwear in drawers.

Sorry, I say, even though I want to say it wasn't too loud before you came in the damn room.

I suddenly feel really angry at Mom for being in here at all, and I shut my eyes tight and clench my fists.

So the party was fun? she says, all perky.

It was fine, I say, sort of through my teeth, but there's just no way Mom's going to think I might not possibly want to talk about it.

What did you all do?

I want to say, Spin the Bottle and Pin the Tail on the Stoner, Mom.

Not too much, I say.

It was so nice of Alexandra to invite you, she says, chirpy, like a canary really, and I kind of want to scream.

Yeah, I say.

It would be nice if you could start going places with her, she says. Every girl should have one really good girlfriend.

Yeah, I say, and then I think about Alexandra blowing tobacco in my face.

Someone to go to the movies with, to talk to on the phone, Mom says.

I open my eyes and look over at her, and she's just sort of standing there, looking all dreamy, and I think maybe I should tell her *she* should go hang out with Alexandra Stuart.

Then she picks up my jeans and says, Doreen, what happened to these? They have stains all over them.

I slipped on the lawn last night, I say, and Mom looks at me.

Well, you can't wear them out like this. Only wear this pair around the house.

I want to say, But what should I wear to opening night at the opera?

Yeah, OK, I say.

What's this, Mom says then, and I look up.

She's holding the letter I stole from Alexandra's drawer, turning it over in her hands a couple of times.

Oh, it's, um, it's mine, I say.

Did you write a letter to Alexandra? she says, perky beyond belief.

Yeah, I say. I just—thanked her and stuff, I say.

Oh, Mom says, and she gets all bright. Well, that's very nice, Doreen.

Then she hands me the letter and sort of pats me on the shoulder and she leaves, and I'm pretty thankful. Yeah, Mom, Alexandra's nice, I'm nice—everyone's so nice we don't know what to do with ourselves.

I look at the letter, and I can't believe I forgot about it, but I guess it probably wasn't the most important thing that happened last night.

I open the envelope real carefully, and I pull the letter out. It's just this crappy piece of binder paper ripped out of a notebook, and the first thing I look at is the last line: "I'll always love you, Alexandra. Love, Alex."

Then I read the whole thing twice and giggle, and I lean back on my bed and laugh my ass off and almost cry because it's all so perfect, and it really amazes me how everything's so shitty one second and then the next second—perfect.

Shit, Doreen, you're really fuckin' crazy, Ted says to me on our way out of Kinko's.

But I don't even think about that. I just start walking real fast, holding the papers in my hand.

Ted's giggling all excited, like we're six years old and about to get on Space Mountain. He keeps looking around us as if there are people listening in on everything we say. I don't even care. Suddenly, I wouldn't even care if we were on stage at the damn Hollywood Bowl.

I can't believe this, Ted whispers, and then he laughs some more.

Me, I don't say anything. I don't even want to smile until it's all done.

How did you even think of this? Ted says to me, amazed, like I just came up with the cure for cancer.

How did you not? I say, and it's true.

Nothing is ever so easy.

Then I stop walking, and I figure we better get started.

Here? Ted says.

We've got to start somewhere, I say, and I pull one of the sheets from my stack.

Ted shrugs, and then he takes off his backpack and pulls out the staple gun that was lying around his basement somewhere, which his mom has for God knows whatever reason. He holds it up like a trophy, all proud and smiley.

Here, he says, and he hands me the staple gun, and then he pulls out this old-looking camera.

What's that for?

I want to remember this forever, he says. Go ahead.

You're such a dork, I mutter, but then I laugh a little, because I am kind of happy he brought the camera.

It's like this—I know pictures get wrinkled and old, and usually they don't really capture the way things really happened, but it's still kind of nice to have them around. Because then you can look at them and remember, even if you say to yourself, Oh, it wasn't like that at all that day. You still think about that day.

And Mom has kept all these pictures of me and Tracey, and every Christmas, she sends out these lame family portraits to everyone she's ever met, and me and Tracey and Mom and Dad are all sitting in the living room looking like tools, because we never all sit together like that. I'm sure everyone just tosses those bullshit pictures, except for maybe Uncle Bill and Aunt Shirley who stick it on their fridge for like, a week, until they throw it out with the damn Christmas tree.

But on the other hand, I would give anything—my thumbs, my CDs, Dave Campos's left one, if I could get one cruddy, smashed-up picture of Henry. Just one.

Come on, Ted says, and he lifts the camera and shuts one eye.

I put the sheet of paper on the telephone pole in front of us, and then I lift the staple gun and press and shoot, and it kachunks and snaps back in my hand, sort of.

Stand next to it, Ted says.

Huh?

Huh? Ted says, making a face, imitating me. Let me get a shot of you standing next to the first one, he says, waving me over.

I stand next to the pole and the sheet I just staple-gunned to it, and Ted snaps about ten pictures. I'm about to get real annoyed with him until I see how happy it's making him, and then I look at the stack of papers in my hand and I can't help but laugh too. I don't want to show off or anything, but I think this is kind of the coolest thing we've ever done. It may be the coolest thing anyone's ever done.

You next, I say, and I hand him the staple gun, and he hands me the camera.

He stands next to the pole, and I snap a couple of Ted and his goofy smile. He's so proud of this, and I guess I am too. I take the camera away from my face, and I look at the Xeroxed paper with my writing scrawled across the top of it: DIRTY WORDS, and there's an arrow pointing down, pointing to the letter.

Dear Alexandra,

I'm sorry I yelled last night. That was pretty wack. It's just like, I was real mad, but not mad at you like that. I was just mad at myself I think, because I was frustrated with shit. I know that it was not your fault. I just wanted to sleep with with you so bad and be the 1st and so I thought you were all tight and pissed because you didn't want to sleep with me as well. Then I talked to Dave about everything and I chilled. I mean, that's real fucked up of me I think. Again I'm sorry. I can't say it enough. I'll always love you, Alexandra.

Love, Alex

Let's find another one, Ted says, and then he sort of squeals.

I nod, and then we start walking again. Neither of us are saying anything, but we keep looking at each other and cracking up. And we keep walking faster and faster and looking at each other and busting up, even though it takes the wind out of us and hurts our throats because it's so hot.

And then me and Ted run like we never had any business walking. We just keep running, from corner to corner, pole to pole. We staple copies of the letter everywhere: by Tower, by the square, by the 7-Eleven and the Trader Joe's, in our neighborhood and on Altamont Avenue and all through Old Town.

The whole time I'm humming "Oh My Golly" and singing the parts I know, and Ted's singing with me, and we hardly talk even.

Ro-sa . . . Ro-oh-oh-oh-oh-SA . . .

It's like my and Ted's anthem today, even though most of the words are in Spanish and we don't know what the hell it means, but that doesn't matter. It just doesn't.

I'm so hyped up when I get home that I don't even notice Matthew's car in the driveway at first. I mean, I see it and everything, but it doesn't really register that he's probably right inside. And then I think about it—and the chill comes over me again and I can't breathe for a second, and then I can't get inside fast enough.

I go in, and he's there, standing next to Tracey, who's talking to Mom, but he looks over at me when I come in, and then he looks away again. I guess he doesn't want to be too obvious about any-thing. Tracey's talking at Mom, trying to convince her to let her do something stupid, and Mom just keeps going, Ask your father, ask your father.

I just stand there and look at Matthew because I think he'll look over at me and wink or something the way he does, but he doesn't. He sort of looks down at his shoes and my heart starts beating faster when I think about his hands on my face last night and then I start sweating even though the air conditioning's on.

Doreen, you're so flushed, Mom says.

Yeah, well, I ran from Ted's, I say before I realize how dumb it sounds.

Tracey looks at me all annoyed, like I have some kind of nerve for talking while she's asking Mom for something so important, like if she can borrow the car and not come home till tomorrow.

Mom, you guys don't need the car tonight, she whines. I wouldn't ask you, but it's just that Matthew's loaning his car to a friend of his.

Matthew's standing there, not looking at me, not even acting like he knows I'm there at all.

It's a little weird.

Well, why can't Susan pick you two up? Mom says to Tracey.

Mom, we're not babies, Tracey says, all rude. I really don't wanna have to *carpool*.

Mom starts to get all fluttery and turns around and starts wiping the counter with a rag.

What do you need it for, though? Mom says, kind of quiet.

Tracey exhales all loud and says, We're just going to Sam's mom's place in Brentwood.

I guess that's kind of a better answer instead of Actually, Mom, me and all of my stupid friends are planning to take about nine hits of acid and drive around and listen to the same song over and over again while we try to talk to Jesus through the sunroof.

You're going to have to ask your father, Mom says for the thousandth time, and then she takes the garbage out from underneath the sink and starts wrapping it up to take it out to the curb even though it's practically empty and there's just, like, a paper towel in it.

Then she leaves, and I look back at Tracey and Tracey says, What the fuck do you want?

Then I look at Matthew because I want him to look over at me so bad I could scream, but he doesn't. It's like I'm not even there, and I look back at Tracey, all angry at everything, and then she leaves and Matthew follows her to her room and doesn't look back at me.

There's this tied-up ball in my stomach and I feel like I just swallowed a bunch of rocks, and I breathe real hard for a second and then I head for my room. I can hear Matthew's voice through Tracey's door on the way, and I kind of slam the door behind me and then I put on Bossanova and blast it and I start chewing my fingernails a little bit.

It's not a really bad habit I have—I don't chew on them that much, especially when I smoke with Ted, but right now I work my thumbnail like someone's paying me to do it, chewing it all around the edges and ripping the pieces with my teeth like they're little bits of bone and I get to gnawing on my skin even and ripping it a little so it's peeling off my thumb in shreds and it's soft and gummy and salty in my mouth and then I guess I bite a little too hard because my thumb starts bleeding and then I end up just sitting on my floor,

leaning against the door, sucking my thumb and listening to loud
music.

There's always all this sweat on the inside of my knees and elbows
and armpits—those are the places where I'm mostly sweating all the
time. And then as soon as I walk outside or twist around in my bed,
I can feel it get all damp on my forehead and my back, and then it's
all over. Then even my *eyelids* are sweating. Then I'm all wet no matter what.

I try to go to sleep because I know Ted's going to call and he's
going to want to rehash everything about today, and I just don't feel
like it. He's going to want to talk about it over and over, and I can
just hear his dumb excited voice saying remember this remember
that, and I don't want to have to pretend to be all excited with him. I
mean, I had a good time and everything—it was even better than that,
I guess. It was like I had won a contest or something, but that's all
gone now.

Now I'm just lying around, trying to spread out my arms and legs
from my body so they don't get all sweaty and sticky, but that's just
stupid anyway. There's no way around sweating out, like, ten liters a
day around here. And I can't figure Matthew out. I can't believe he
could pay so much attention to a person, make a person feel all great,
and then he just wouldn't even so much as look at me today. I bet he
hates me. I bet he thinks I'm stupid and dorky and ugly.

I turn over on my side and stare at Kim Deal. It's the poster of the
inside of *Bossanova* where she's smiling all wide and looks a little
blurry. I think about how maybe Matthew lied when he said he liked

the Pixies. Maybe he just felt like pretending. Maybe he planned the whole thing with Tracey. Maybe they're laughing about it right now. It's probably the best joke they've ever played. I swear I can hear Tracey's voice and her annoying laugh:

You didn't think he actually *liked* you, did you?

I bury my face in the pillow so I can hardly breathe and I say Fuck Tracey Fuck Tracey Fuck Tracey over and over again until they're just nonsense words. I can feel myself almost start to cry and then I cough a little and say to myself, Fuck you. I hate it when people cry.

Fuck Tracey. Fuck Matthew. Fuck Mom and Dad. Fuck family. Fuck this house. Fuck the cool kids. Fuck rich assholes. Fuck famous people. Fuck commercials. Fuck whiners. Fuck everyone who's in a fucking band. Fuck scenesters. Fuck druggies. Fuck pretty. Fuck Top fucking 40. Fuck rolling with the fucking punches. Fuck models. Fuck idiots. Fuck school. Fuck perfume. Fuck lipstick. Fuck Pasadena. Fuck on time. Fuck hip alternative soundtracks. Fuck everyone who's full of shit. Fuck spending hours constructively. Fuck married people and fuck in love people and fuck dating people. And fuck people who whine about no one wanting to date them. Fuck summer. Fuck heat. Fuck sweat. Fuck every fucking owner of every store who looks at kids like they're stealing all the time. Fuck M fucking TV. Fuck easy listening. Fuck club kids and fuck ravers and skaters and hippies. Fuck all the people who just get stuff, who always have and always will. Fuck liars and fuck people who pretend they never lie. Fuck people who leave. Fuck board games. Fuck boredom. Fuck happy people. Fuck boys who shit on girls and fuck girls who love it. Fuck pussy no balls chicken shits. Fuck this fucking city and this fucking block and fuck this fucking world and fuck all its everything.

And fuck you too.

I'm having this dream where I'm in some bar and I order chocolate milk, and the guy behind the bar says, On the rocks? and I say yeah. On the rocks. There's all these old people sitting around me, and there's this old Chinese lady with no teeth who's sort of trying to tickle me, I think. For some reason, it really freaks the hell out of me. The old Chinese lady is really scary, and I try to gulp for air and breathe, and the old Chinese lady's grabbing my arm hard now, and I wake up real quick, like I've been thrown in a pool of cold water or something.

I don't even know how it started. You can never tell how anything is when you just wake up like that.

I don't even know how it started. Now even. Even when I think hard about it. Even when I close my eyes and don't breathe and all I see is black. Even when I turn onto my stomach and stick my face in my pillow. Even when I shut my window so I can't even hear a car go by now and again. Even then I can't remember.

I don't really know how it started. All I know is. All I know is nothing. All I know is there were rumors. All I know is that I didn't want to open my eyes really. All I know is I couldn't move. All I know is I still don't think I can move. All I know is there's a big tear now and every time I close my eyes I think I can hear it happening—like a thousand pieces of paper being ripped in half.

I was looking at the shadows on my ceiling from the cars that drove by once in a while. Either I was looking at that or my eyes were closed. Or covered. I don't know. I can't remember now.

I was so hot the whole time. Burning right up. I could feel the sweat on my back seeping through the sheets. My mouth was dry, and I felt like all my bones were creaking like a rusty bicycle every time I moved. But I didn't actually move all that much. I didn't know what I should do. It was easier having my eyes covered, I think. I think staring at a bunch of black was easier. It sort of made me feel like I was in space or something. It helped because I didn't know anything about anything. Sometimes it helps for someone to cover your eyes because that way you don't have to see if you're doing anything wrong.

I wasn't scared or anything. I just didn't know what I was doing. It's hard to know what from what when you're woken up like that. You practically don't know your own name even when you're woken up like that.

Doreen Doreen Doreen. I kept thinking that, actually. It's pretty weird to hear your own name over and over and over again. You're such a nice girl, Doreen. He was in my ear practically. And when I hurt so bad like someone was stabbing me I opened my mouth to say shit or something, he covered my mouth too. Shhh. You're so perfect, Doreen. I kept thinking then the devil is sex then the devil is sex. That's what I thought it was until I got the CD and saw it was then the devil is six and then I really didn't know what the hell it meant.

I thought of Tracey, actually. I don't know what I should have been thinking of, but I thought of Tracey and that was pretty weird of me. I thought how she did this too sometime, whenever it was. She didn't tell me about it or anything, but sometime she was all stupid and didn't know anything like me and some guy put his hands all over her eyes and mouth and she felt like she was in space and she got all torn up too. But then I think she was probably drunk or tripping or something. She probably said some stupid fucking thing like what's up with this. What's up with this guy on top of me.

That makes me laugh.

Hey. Been trying to meet you. Hey. Must be a devil between us.

I kept thinking that too. Hey. It's like I'm not even here. I feel small. Short. Like a midget almost. Then I started thinking about what if I was a midget. Then I laughed because it was such a goofy thing to think about. I kept laughing, thinking Matthew probably wouldn't be fucking me if I was a midget. If I was a midget, Matthew wouldn't be on top of me, and this wouldn't be happening. I know it sounds crazy, but that's what I was thinking. I swear.

I look at my hands, and almost all of my fingernails are broken, and I wonder how the hell that happened. There's also all this dirt under them, and I don't know how that happened either, but it's like I've been climbing up the side of a cliff or something.

Thinking about it now, I think it probably wasn't so bad. I think I probably made it worse somehow, because I'm always doing stupid shit like that. I'm always making a situation worse because I never pay attention to anything for very long. Mom's always saying how I'm in my own world, and she's right about it. I decide I should probably go to sleep but I won't let myself until I make a promise to start paying attention to things. So I do. I promise.

Then I still can't sleep.

I stuff the sheets in the Dumpster behind the 7-Eleven the next morning. I don't know what I'll say to Mom when she asks what happened to them, but I don't much care. They're just sheets. I mean, they're not worth a thousand dollars or anything. Still and all, she's probably going to wonder. I guess I would.

I close the lid over them, and it makes this snapping sound when it hits the base. It sort of makes me jump. I feel pretty jumpy on the whole, actually. When I was coming here with the sheets all balled up in my backpack, I felt like everyone in every car that passed knew what I had. I know that's stupid. I know they probably weren't even looking at me, but that's what I mean when I say I'm really jumpy. I mean, normally I don't think everyone cares about my business, so why should they today?

I look around me in the parking lot, and no one's here at all, but I just feel eyes coming out of the ground or something—all staring up at me as I step on them. Squishing under my toes. I feel like I don't know what to do.

I figure I better go home sooner or later and take a shower and stuff, but it makes me kind of sick inside to think about doing that. Then I think maybe I should go to Ted's, but he won't know anything, and he'll still want to talk about yesterday and all that shit, and I just don't want to deal. It sort of makes me feel sick thinking about Ted too for some reason, and I have to sit down for a second.

The back of my head feels real hot, and all of a sudden it's like I can't breathe and my mouth gets all full of spit, so I open my mouth to spit on the ground in front of me, but instead I puke. I puke so hard and so long it comes out of my nose even. Then the smell hits me, and that makes me puke some more, and then it finally stops, and my throat hurts, and I lean back and my throw-up's all yellow, and it's practically melting on the asphalt, and flies start circling.

Hey, somebody says to me.

I look up, and it's the guy who runs the 7-Eleven, who's always looking at me funny.

Hey, you can no do that here, he says with some accent, pointing his bony finger at me.

I . . . uh, is all I can say, because I'm kind of dizzy, and my mouth tastes disgusting.

You get drunk somewhere else, he says all angry, and he fixes his eyes on me like I'm a criminal in a lineup. Of course I can't see him too clearly because his hair's so shiny from whatever kind of Crisco shortening hair oil he uses, it's practically blinding me.

I didn't mean to throw up on your lot, mister, I say.

You are here before, he says, recognizing me.

Yeah, I'm the troublemaker who buys Tiger's Milk Bars and Cola—I'm really a menace to society.

Why not you leave now? he says, crossing his arms.

Why not you *wash your fucking hair?!?* I bark at him, and he starts screaming in some crazy language, so I get up and start running.

I don't exactly have lots of energy, since I can't remember the last time I ate, and I just barfed whatever it was up anyway. Truth is, I have no idea where I'm going, but I run anyway, until my legs hurt, and then I sit down on the curb and lie back and close my eyes. And I hear a million flies buzzing around my head, and I still smell dried puke all over me, and maybe I fall asleep for a second or what, I don't know. All I know is when I open my eyes, there's some old guy standing in front of me.

He says something to me but I don't really hear it, so I say, What? and my mouth is all dry.

Are you OK? he says in his scratchy old-guy voice.

I shrug, trying to act all cool, which is pretty stupid seeing that I'm collapsed on the fucking sidewalk.

Do you want some water, he says.

I shrug again and say, I'm OK.

You don't look OK, missy, he says.

Missy. That's an old people thing. Gram used to call Mom and Aunt Shirley Missy. But who does this guy think he is? Teachers, Mom, everyone practically, try to carve into little girls' foreheads how we're not supposed to talk to strangers, especially sketchy old guys with spots all over their heads, and this guy's trying to chat it up.

Well, I am, I say.

Then stand up and get off my property, he says.

You own the sidewalk? I say, all bratty.

No, but I own that lawn, and it looks to be your knapsack on it, he says, just as bratty as me, actually—I'm almost proud of the old guy.

I turn my head, and there's my backpack in a sad heap on his lawn, and I guess it fell off my shoulder when I lied down.

Fine, I say, and I try to stand up a little, sort of balancing on my haunches like a bunny or something, but then I see a bunch of flashes out of the corner of my eye, like someone's snapping a million pictures, and I can't feel my legs for a second. I fall back down on my ass and the rest of me snaps back too.

My head's on its way straight to the concrete when I feel the old guy's hands on my shoulders. His hands are big and strong, like he's wearing baseball gloves or something, and he holds me up.

Come on now, I hear him say. I'll help you stand.

I don't need help, I try to say, but the words come out all weird.

Come on, he says. He pulls me to my feet, and I feel his hands under my shoulders, in my armpits, but I still feel like a puppet, and the flashes start again, and the last thing I see is the sky, which is as blue and clear as painted glass.

When I open my eyes, I think I'm dreaming, I swear. I'm lying on some couch that makes noises when I turn around, and there's wallpaper with flowers on it, and it's all brown and yellow and old, and there's a brown Formica coffee table with this fake gold trim along the edges. I look up at this clock on the wall that is pointy and gold and for a second I think maybe I'm in the '50s. I mean, I don't really think I'm in the '50s but it looks like that from here.

Then I remember the parking lot at 7-Eleven and puking and falling asleep on the sidewalk and the old guy. And then the old guy comes in with a tray.

How are you feeling? he says to me, not looking at me, just putting the tray on the coffee table.

Fine, I say, lying as stiff as a board, thinking please don't be a pervert please don't be a pervert please please please.

You took quite a spill out there, he says, and I see that he's made me a sandwich. Crusts cut off. There's also a glass of water.

Yeah, I guess.

No guessing about it, he says. Here, have some water.

I'm really kind of nervous to take the water because I've heard stories about guys who give girls drinks spiked with all kinds of shit to make them pass out, but I figure the old guy could've already done whatever he wanted to me, and he didn't. At least I think he didn't. At this point, though, I'm so thirsty I could die, so I don't much care what's in the water.

I take it and drink it all down, and I feel some dribbling down my chin, and I wipe it and I figure the old guy must think I'm such a slob.

It'll do good for you to eat something, he says, and he pushes the sandwich toward me.

No, that's OK, I say, my voice cracking and sounding all dumb.

When's the last time you ate? he says.

I shrug. He must think I'm a homeless person or something. A homeless slob.

It's peanut butter and jelly, he says, holding the plate out, and I almost laugh because this is all so weird.

My mouth waters a little, and I just nod so I won't start drooling, and so he won't think I'm some maniac.

I take a half of the sandwich and bite into it, and I could almost cry, it's so good. The peanut butter's really smooth and sugary, not like that healthy, chunky kind my mom's so crazy about. I don't know why anyone would want peanut butter to taste like a bunch of sand. And the jelly's pretty perfect too. It's not that grainy jam with little hard things floating around that get stuck between your teeth— it's real jelly.

I don't really know it, but I'm sort of inhaling the sandwich, and I almost choke.

Easy now, says the old guy, and I see that his eyes are all blood-shot, and I think maybe he's a drug addict.

I saw this movie once, where this old guy who was a doctor kept all these drugs in his refrigerator, and he was all smacked out all the time.

Are you a doctor? I say to the old guy with my mouth full.

No, ma'am, he says. It doesn't take a doctor to see you need food and water.

I don't tell him that's not why I wanted to know. Believe me, old guy, I don't think you're some kind of genius for giving me a PB&J. I just thought you were a junkie is all.

What's your name, missy? he says.

It sure as hell isn't Missy, I'm about to say, but the old guy's been pretty nice to me. I don't need to be all rude just because I feel like it.

Doreen, I say.

My name's Frank, he says, and he holds out his hand for me to shake it, and I do, and it's all pruney and sweaty.

You'd best call your folks and tell them to come get you, he says.

No, I say, a little too loudly.

Well, why not? They should know you fainted on my front lawn, he says.

It's just that I don't have any parents, I say.

He scrunches up his forehead and keeps looking at me with those hound dog eyes.

They're dead.

He looks down and seems really sad. I don't even know why he should be, though. He just met me and everything.

I'm real sorry about that, he says, and I feel kind of guilty for making him feel so bad.

Who looks after you then? he asks.

My brother, Henry.

We should give him a call, then. Tell him to come fetch you.

He's not home, I say. He's working.

Can you call him at work?

I almost start laughing because the old guy believes me. I guess he doesn't have a reason not to—it's just that whenever I lie, I mostly feel like everyone knows. But I feel pretty cool making the old guy believe what I say. I mean Christ, I'm an orphan. Everybody believes orphans.

Where does he work?

Um . . . in a warehouse, I say.

Is there a phone there? he says, wrinkling up his forehead, and I think maybe he's not believing me so much anymore.

Yeah, but hey, his bosses get kind of angry when I call, I say real fast.

The old guy nods and stands up.

Well, Doreen, I don't quite feel right letting you walk home. You've fainted twice, and you would've hurt your head badly if I hadn't caught you.

I sort of wince when he says my name like that. Sometimes I get all weird when I hear my name. Who knows why.

I'd feel a lot better if I drove you home, he says, putting his hands in his pockets and jingling his keys. Or maybe it's change. He seems like the kind of old guy who'd have a lot of stuff in his pockets.

No, it's really OK. I mean, thanks for everything, but I feel a lot better now. I really think I can walk it, I say, because I don't know what I'd say to Mom if she saw me getting out of some strange man's Oldsmobile.

I'm afraid I just can't let you do that, he says.

I sort of start to get freaked out a little. Maybe he is some crazed junkie who's going to sell me off to get more drugs. Or maybe he lures kids into his house and gives them peanut butter and jelly right before he hacks them up into bits.

I must look kind of nervous, because then he says, Tell you what, Doreen, why don't I give you some money, and I'll call you a taxi.

I don't say anything, and then when I finally speak, my voice cracks again, and I sound all stupid.

How would I pay you back, though?

Let's not worry about that, he says, pulling this ancient phone book out of a drawer. Then, without looking up at me, he says, If it would make you feel better, you can send the money back to me.

Thanks, I say quietly, so quietly that I can hardly hear myself, even.

When the taxi comes, I tell him to let me out after we go for about two blocks, and then I take the rest of the fifteen bucks the old guy gave me and I go to Trader Joe's, and I buy two bags of chocolate mint UFO candies. Then I go to some corner store, and I buy four Tiger's Milk Bars and a bottle of Coke and a big bag of barbecue chips, and I sit on the curb in front of the store and eat all the Tiger's Milk Bars and about half the bag of chips, and I start in on one of the bags of the chocolate mints but then I stop because I feel gross again. I don't throw up even though I feel like I'm going to, and I just walk around and drink the Coke and burp a lot and before I even notice, it's getting dark, and I start to head home.

When I walk through the door, everything's really quiet. Or at least it seems really quiet, probably because the TV's not on. The light's off in the living room too, which is weird. It doesn't make much sense that no one would be home. Mom should be making dinner, and Dad should be sitting around not saying anything.

I start to walk to my room, and I peek into the kitchen, and Mom and Dad are both staring at me like zombies. Mom's eyes are all red like she's been crying, and at first I think maybe there's been an accident, that maybe somebody died or something, and I get kind of excited inside when I think about that. It's sort of a sick thing with

me. I sort of can't wait to hear bad news and all the details sometimes. I wonder if maybe something happened to Tracey, and maybe
we'll all have to go to the hospital and stay there all night, and I start
thinking about calling Ted from the emergency room, but then I look
at Dad, and I feel dead for a second.

Dad looks like his head's about to pop off his neck he's so angry
and he's standing behind Mom, gripping onto the chair she's sitting
in, and I know it's me.

Where have you been? he says really slowly and quietly, breathing before he says each word, it seems like.

I've been at Ted's, I say, and my voice sounds really small.

Ted's called here five times looking for you, Mom says, all
choked up, and then tears start pouring down her face and I fucking
hate that. I really hate it when people cry.

Don't lie, Dad says. Where have you been?

Out, I say.

Out where? Dad says.

Walking around, I say, and I start walking to my room because I
just can't believe this is that big a deal.

With who? Dad fires back, and I hear him following me. I want to
say, With my new crack dealer friends, and then they all *gangbanged*
me, and they're *black,* and *I liked it,* Daddy.

With no one.

Then I feel Dad's hand on my arm like it's a claw and he whirls
me around so quick I think my arm's going to snap off, and he gets
right up in my face and says, You're grounded.

I can't even look at him when he's like this—his eyes get all crazy, and he starts to walk back down the hall, and Mom comes out of the kitchen to say something to him, I guess, and all that chocolate's made me jumpy and I have this headache that won't go away and I get so angry that I want to shout *fuck you,* but instead I shout,

That's *real fair, Dad!!!* and both of them stare at me, and then Dad practically sprints down the hall and grabs my arm again.

You will watch your mouth, he says, all calm and weird, like he's a robot, and then he opens the door to my room and sort of tosses me in there.

Even though I'm taller than Mom and Tracey, Dad's still a lot taller and stronger than me, and when he jerks me into the room I fall against my bed and hit my shin on the frame. It really hurts, but I just sit there and stare at Dad, and my hair's all in my face, and I'm in such pain and so angry I'm shaking.

You will stay in here until I tell you to come out, he says in the calm robot voice again.

Mom appears in the doorway and grabs onto Dad's arm for a second but he shakes her off like a fly. She's all shivery and pale and teary, and I hate her so much. She's so goddamn stupid. I hate it when people cry all the time. As if it helps. As if it *does* anything.

Mom doesn't seem to be looking at me, though. She's sort of looking past me, and I stop staring at Dad so I can turn around. My bare bed. Then I turn back to them, and Mom's shaking so hard I think maybe she'll crack like an egg if I'm lucky maybe. If I'm lucky maybe they'll both just crack into a million pieces on the hall carpet. Mom bites her lip and at first I think she's going to start crying all loud again but instead she wails,

Where are your sheets?!

Then she falls against the wall, all weepy, like the sheets mean more than the house or something.

I think they're ugly, I say. I threw them away.

Mom doesn't even look at me, and I don't look at her either. I just stare at Dad and he stares back at me and neither of us blink and my eyes start to feel raw like they're going to fall out and, for a second, I wonder if Dad's are too. He's as red as a beet and, when he opens his mouth, I almost expect fire to come out of it or an earthquake to start or something. But he stares at me just the same and says to Mom, She can sleep on the mattress.

Then he shuts the door on me and I hear them walking to their room. I kind of giggle thinking about it—She can sleep on the mattress. Maybe later he'll make me clean out the chimney and sell matchbooks on the street and I hope I get home before I turn into a damn *pumpkin*. Jesus. Christ. On. His. Throne.

I'm still shaking, but I don't know if it's from the chocolate or from being pissed off or what. My shin hurts pretty bad, and I pull up my jeans a little but then I see this weird crusty dirt on my sock. I take off my shoes, and the dirt's all over my feet, not just on the bottom which usually gets all gross. I scratch at it a little, and it flakes off my sock and onto the carpet. It's like dried mud or something.

Then I see it's on my calves too, and I sort of scratch it off a little, but then I see that it reaches up to near my knees too, so I just take off my jeans to see. There are lines of brown all the way up to my underwear. I pull off my underwear too, and I put my fingers up myself for a second, just to see. It stings really bad still, and I pull my fingers out and there's blood on them and it's different. It's not all thick and gross like it is when I have my period. I hate having my period, dripping all over the place. But this isn't like that. It's really thin, like when I cut myself shaving. Not that I shave that often because I can't really do it very well—I'm always scabbing up my legs. But that's what this is like. I kind of wish I could wash myself off, but I don't think I should leave my room.

So I decide to leave myself like that, all crusty and scabby. It's pretty gross, but I think why should I take a shower when I'm bleeding so steady? And anyway, I'm just going to get sweaty all over again.

I can't fall asleep, which seems weird to me because I really haven't slept much lately at all. I mean, I did faint and everything, but I don't think that actually counts. And I think fainting sort of makes you tired, which is weird. I was pretty tired at the old guy's house, pretty groggy and dim, but not now. Maybe I just want to be tired so I can have something to do, even if it is just taking a nap. Being locked in my room isn't exactly a great time. I guess there's nothing I'd really rather be doing though. Except maybe be at Ted's. He called five times. He probably thinks I'm dead in a gutter somewhere. Maybe he thinks I ran off. Who knows what he thinks. Maybe he didn't worry at all and he's just bored. That's so like Ted to call five times. He knows damn well I always call him back, so I don't know what the big idea is.

I hate it when people do that, when people just call and call. One of Tracey's dumb friends, Sam, used to do that and it used to really annoy me. It's like, no, dumbass, Tracey hasn't gotten home in the last five seconds—why don't you get a hobby?

I get up and put on *Come On, Pilgrim* and I lie back down and think there's no way I'll fall asleep with the Pixies screaming in my ear. I've always loved Black Francis's voice. I think because he just freaks out and screams so much. Everything's going along just fine, Kim's thumping on the bass all steady and smooth, and then he'll just lose his shit and start screaming. I love that. I close my eyes and listen to "The Holiday Song." My favorite line is when he says, They kissed till they were dead. It makes me think of two people kissing so hard they practically bite each other's lips off. People gnawing and biting at each other, digging their nails into each other's skin.

I think of Matthew. I think of him biting my bottom lip and yanking it. I think of his hand over my eyes. Every time I close my eyes I see him on top of me, over me. I see how his face was. He was sort of like some strange guy I never met before. I mean, he's strange anyway, but he wasn't talking like him. He wasn't smiling at me or winking—he didn't even look at me really. And I didn't look that much anyway, so what do I know? But he was different. It's like I didn't know who the real Matthew was, and this was just some weird sex guy.

I start to feel kind of sick thinking about everything and probably because I ate all that shit, so I turn up the music even louder so I don't have to think about anything, and that's the great thing about music. Usually, my head gets all jammed up all the time, but when I put music on, I don't have to think about anything. I really love that.

It sounds like it's all around me and for a second I think maybe if I open my eyes, the Pixies will be right there. That would be cool except I'd have no idea what to say and I'd probably end up sounding like an idiot. Rock n Roll forever.

I wake up to what sounds like rain, but it hasn't rained around here in so long so I know that can't be right. My stereo's humming because the CD's been over but I don't know for how long. I try to ignore the rain sound but it just keeps going. *Tap Tap Tap.* I think I'm dreaming, maybe, and it just doesn't stop. It sounds more like a faucet dripping. Yeah, one of those faucets that just suspend in midair, Dor, I think to myself and I get more awake and kneel on my bed and I see a little hand tapping.

I slide the window open and stick my head out.

What the fuck are you doing? I say to Ted.

I can't really see him because the light from my room doesn't really make it out the window, and he's sort of crouching down anyway, but I can still tell it's him. I don't know who else it would be.

Your Mom didn't know where you were when I called, he whispers.

What time is it? I say, squinting to try and see his eyes, but I still can't. It's kind of hard to talk to someone when you can barely see them.

It's like, eleven, he says, even quieter.

You don't have to whisper, I say. My parents can't really hear from this side.

Oh. OK, he says, but he's still being all quiet.

We've got to talk, he says all serious, like he knows something I don't. I hate it when he gets like this. I feel like laughing, but I don't because then he'd get all pissy.

What's wrong with you?

Can you just come down here, please?

Fine, I say, kind of huffy.

I go to put on my shoes and stuff, and I don't know why I'm acting all annoyed. I hate it when I'm in my room for a long time, and it's weird, I don't feel like I have to sleep at all suddenly.

I poke my head out of the window and tell Ted to move out of the way. I haven't done this in a long time, and I guess I'm bigger now, because it's not so easy. I hold onto the top rim of the windowpane and try to stick my legs through the window, but they bang against the sides and the bruise on my shin hurts real bad. It's like I have way too many limbs—all of a sudden I feel like a giant octopus or something trying to get through.

Do you want me to catch you? Ted whispers up to me.

Get out of the way, I say, and I wriggle my hips through, which isn't exactly easy either.

I start to fall through and my shirt hikes up on the bottom rim and my back gets all skinned. Ted still doesn't get out of the way, as if he's going to catch me, as if I don't outweigh him by like, thirty pounds. I sort of yelp a little and then I fall, and it's not a very big fall, only a few feet really, and Ted's standing there with his arms open like an idiot, so I totally crush him and we fall into a heap against the side of my house.

Ow ow ow, Ted says underneath me, all crunched up like an accordion.

I told you to get out of the way, I say, and I push his head.

Ow ow, he says, grabbing the side of his head, curling up even more.

Oh, come on, you baby, I say. I didn't hit you that hard.

Ted doesn't say anything and stands up and takes my hand and pulls me up and he's still holding his face like a freak and sort of running. We run away from my house and down the street, not in the direction of anything, really.

What is your problem? I say.

He stops all dramatically, and he still won't turn around and look at me.

Jesus, I say, all out of breath, and I sit down on the curb, sort of leaning against the streetlight.

Then Ted looks at me, and I can feel my mouth sort of hang open, and I feel this tingling at the back of my neck and on the back of my legs, all the way up and down when I see. When I see Ted's got these bruises on his face—all brown and blue—by his eye, on his cheek near his ear—there's even this scab near his mouth.

What, what . . . , is all I can say.

I heard someone in the backyard last night so I went out there, he says, looking down. I thought it was probably you.

When he says that, I feel my throat get all tight.

They were all fucking drunk, he says, leaning against the streetlight.

Who? I say, standing up, clenching my fists and my jaw. *Who?* I shout.

Who do you think? Ted shouts back at me, crying all of a sudden. Alex and Dave and Peter . . . and Girl Alex stood there and watched.

He's really crying now and shaking. And I start shaking and I turn around and look up because I don't think I can look at Ted.

Motherfucking shit, I say, stomping my feet like I might explode soon, and I squat on the sidewalk and hug my knees to my chest.

Ted sits down on the curb next to me and sniffles. I just let them, he says.

You didn't do anything? I say through my teeth, not looking at him.

Hey, fuck you, Doreen, he whimpers. You wouldn't've done anything either.

That's a *fucking* lie, I yell, looking up and grabbing his arm. I would've been kicking and biting and pulling their goddamn hair out by the *roots*.

It's not my fault, Ted yells at me.

But it is sometimes. Sometimes I think Ted's one of those people who just lets people step all over them. It makes me so angry—angry at all those stupid kids, but more angry at Ted. Which is stupid and wrong, I know, but I can't help it.

You can't just sit there always, I say to him.

Dor, it's not my fault, he whines.

Yes, it is, you fucking faggot, I yell, grabbing him. As long as you let them you're just giving yourself away to them in little bits. They have to learn . . . they have to, I say, but I'm sort of crying now and breathing all jumpy and it's getting hard to talk.

They have to learn they can't do that to people.

Oh, well, great, Ted says. Great, Dor, why don't you just have all of them on you hitting you like crazy, maybe you wouldn't be all cool, he says, all chokey.

Then he stops because he's crying too hard, and the two of us are sitting there like freaks, crying and gulping, not looking at each other. Our breathing slows down and we both start to quiet down and Ted takes out a cigarette and doesn't offer me one. He just lights up.

May I have a cigarette, *please?* I say.

He throws the pack onto my lap.

You are such a bitch sometimes, Ted says after a few minutes.

Hi, have we met? I say to him. Yeah, no shit I'm a bitch—it's the only way you listen to anything I say.

I listen to everything you say.

Well, it's the only way I can make you care.

Whatever, Dor, he says.

He doesn't seem too angry or chokey anymore, but he's still not looking at me—it doesn't even seem like he cares I'm there at all. I don't know why I get so mean to him. I shouldn't be, I guess. I mean, I don't think Ted's ever not offered me a cigarette.

What can we do? Ted says to me as he flips channels.

Something.

Doreen, just forget it, he says.

Forget it? Did you just forget it? I say to him, all pissed. You're pretty incredible, I mean I really have to hand it to you, Ted, if you can look in the goddamn mirror and everything and forget it.

We already got them good with the letter, he says. There's nothing else we can do.

I get up and walk around because Ted's so damn frustrating. He's sitting there looking like he does, watching Nick at Nite, as if he gets the shit kicked out of him every day.

Would you turn off the TV? I say.

Ted clicks it off.

What? he says, all annoyed.

Let's think of something to do to them.

Dor, Ted says, in serious a-dult mode now, looking down like he's giving me a talking-to. He should be smoking a pipe and watching *60 Minutes,* I swear. Dor, there is nothing we can do. Game's over.

Fuck you, I say. This is shit! Have you noticed how you let everyone treat you like shit, and you just lap it up?!

Well, what the hell are you going to do? he says, half-laughing at me. Me and you can't exactly take them on. I mean, how many *bar brawls* have you been in, Doreen? Are you leading a double life I don't know about?

Truth is, I have no idea what to do. I wish I were bigger. And stronger. And a boy, maybe, but only for long enough so that I could kick the teeth out of Alex and Dave and Peter. And Girl Alex too. I don't know why guys are so scared to hit a girl. They probably figured it was my idea, the letter and everything, and they just hammered Ted because he's a boy. Maybe they didn't think that at all. Who knows what they figured.

Just forget it, Ted says.

I can't.

I have.

Bullshit, I say.

Whatever, Dor . . . Can't we just rent *The Legend of Billie Jean* and call it a night?

I can't forget it though, I think. Me and Ted are just going to go in circles anyway. That's all we ever do. I just wish I was big and could beat up anyone I wanted to. People are so stupid—they'll beat you up just because they feel like it.

I keep thinking about this as I walk home, about how they'll take any excuse just to beat someone up or make them feel like an ant. Then I think maybe Ted's right. But I hate that. I mean, I don't really give a flip that everybody hates me, but it's just that they're allowed to treat you so bad—they step over you like you're part of the curb.

I wish Henry was here, and then I'd ask him to kick some weenie fourteen-year-old ass. I bet he would too. Sure, Dor, he'd say, and he'd wink at me and smile and cigarette smoke would drip out of his mouth like water. I bet he'd get some of his badass friends together and do some pummeling. Don't let anyone treat you like that, Ted, he'd say to Ted, putting his hand on his shoulder like a superhero who just saved everything.

Climbing back through the window is even harder than climbing out was. I have to hoist myself up, and my arms aren't that strong, and by the time I get up there they're shaking like crazy. I squeeze my hips in and I don't realize until I'm halfway inside that I should've gone in feetfirst, and then I tumble down onto my bed headfirst and fall on the floor and bang my shin again.

Shit.

I pull up my jeans leg and look at the bruise and scrapes and dried blood. I'm a fucking mess. I look like a goddamn battered wife.

What a freak. I sit on the floor of my room and run my hand over the bruise and I imagine crawling into a screaming hot bath, so hot my skin turns red and sweat pours down every bit of me.

And then I hear footsteps in the hallway, and the sound of his voice all hushed and quiet makes me jump. I crawl like a jackrabbit over to the door and I put my head up against it to listen. Him and Tracey, but I can't hear what they're saying. I can't really hear her at all. I bet she's drunk. His whispers. You're so beautiful, Doreen. You're so perfect, Doreen. I lie on my back next to the door and lift my shirt up. I put my hand on my stomach and trace around my belly button and I close my eyes. Doreen, you've been waiting for this . . . My fingers go around and around, slow little circles on my stomach.

Then I hear Tracey's door open and close, and I can't hear him anymore. I scramble up so I'm on my knees, and I press my ear to the door, but there's nothing. Nothing.

Fuck, I say aloud, probably too loud, and I feel like I want to scream some more dirty words just to hear them, but I don't want to wake up Dad.

Instead, I hit the floor with my fist, right on the knuckles, and it really hurts. I go over to my stereo and turn it on just so there's some noise.

Why'd they have to go in there . . . why didn't Matthew knock on my door at all. Because he hates you, stupid bitch. He's probably saying the same *fucking* thing to Tracey right now. You're so beautiful, Tracey. You're so *perfect*. You're like a supermodel. You're like nature. You're like goddamn stain glass.

Kissing her touching her stomach fucking her. He probably hates me. He just probably needed to get off. Yeah yeah yeah.

I slam my fist down on my dresser, and Henry's balled-up postcard rolls off it onto the floor. I pick it up and uncrumple it and I don't read it—I just look at the picture: Chicago.

I think maybe I could call. I could just see if there's anyone named Henry Severna in Chicago. I mean, he's probably not there. He sent the postcard a long time ago. He could have moved. He probably just passed through. Maybe he even changed his name. And what would I say, anyway? What's going on, Henry? Remember me? I used to be a lot shorter. Will you please come take me please? I have nothing here. Please come take me. Maybe he's changed his name and then we could get married. We wouldn't have to do anything gross—we could just live together and stuff. I feel like there's a pile of electric cords in my gut, hot and wiry. Maybe we'd accidentally kiss for too long sometime. And he'd kick the shit out of everyone who was mean to me. He's warm and dangerous, I just know it. He'd probably scare me a little. What the fuck do you want, he'd say when I call. I want to come see you . . . I can't stand them either. *I hate all of them.* I hope they die. He'd say, I'll come get you. I'll start driving tonight. Grab all you can carry.

I love you, Henry.

I love you, Doreen.

I stick my head out into the hallway, and everything's quiet. I open my door and don't close it and I go down the hallway into the living room and I pick up the phone and dial 411.

This is Maude. What city, please?

Um, Chicago, please.

Area code's 312.

Thanks, um, could you connect me or something? I whisper.

You have to dial Chicago information, she says, all annoyed.

OK, well, how do I do that?

Dial 1-312-555-1212, she says all slowly, like I'm stupid.

Thanks.

Excuse me for never calling Chicago before, bitch. It's not my fault your name's Maude and you have such an exciting career ahead of you being an *operator* and everything.

So I dial the number.

What city? this guy says all loud and quick.

I guess they're even less polite in Chicago.

Chicago?

Henry Severna, I whisper.

Segerna?

No, it's Severna, I say, a little louder. S-E-V-E-R-N-A?

I hear him click away on his operator keyboard, and I picture him sitting in front of a huge screen the size of a wall and then I picture Henry's name flashing like a billboard.

There's no listing, he says.

What?

No listing for Henry Severna, ma'am.

OK, I say, and then I hang up, and I really want to scream, but I don't. I just put my head down on the phone and cry.

Then I feel a hand clamp down on my shoulder. I open my mouth to scream, but then the hand covers it tight. And I know it's him.

It's just me, Doreen, Matthew whispers into my ear.

I shake his hand off me, which is really sweaty by the way, and I turn around and gulp down some snot and he's standing there and he's so wet he looks like he's been in the shower or something.

Why are you crying? he says.

I'm not supposed to be out here, I say, my voice all hoarse. I'm grounded.

That's why you're crying? he asks, sort of laughing all twitchy.

He looks all gross and weird, not like he usually does. All sweaty and pale and strung-out looking.

No, I say.

Who were you calling? he says.

He kind of demands it, actually, which is weird. He doesn't look right. My mouth is still warm and wet from where his hand was, and I get a little nervous for a second, good-nervous, but then I look at him, and it's not good at all. He looks like a crazy person, like some sketchy guy you'd see on TV. Actually, more like some stupid actor playing some sketchy guy—too good-looking to actually be sketchy.

Nobody.

He laughs at me now.

Hey, look, shut up, I say quietly. I'm not supposed to be out here.

So? he says, all rude all of a sudden.

So you're going to get me in trouble.

Since when do you not like trouble? he says, and he stands real close to me, so he's right in my face. There are some people like that, who don't think you're listening to them unless they're right in your face.

He stands so close to me so I can feel the coffee table behind me dig into my calves, and I keep leaning back, away from him, so far I think I might fall and crash through the table.

Huh? he says, breathing against my face.

Then he closes his eyes and breathes deep for a second.

You smell nice, Doreen.

There he is again, with how nice I smell. I know for a fact I don't smell nice because I haven't taken a shower in two days.

No, I don't, I say.

Yeah, you do.

I have to go, I say, slipping away from him.

You don't want to talk to me? he says. Don't you like me any-more, Doreen? he says.

Well, sure, I say, but it's just like, I'm in a lot of trouble right now and I don't need to get in any more.

I look down at my feet. Now I start thinking. This is the first time I've seen him since last night. Last night happened. It's sort of like I can't look at him the same. I mean, he does look like a junkie freak tonight, but that's not why I can't look at him the same. There's this line now, like wire, connecting us and pulling me. My heart starts beating so hard and fast I can feel it at the top of my head.

What's wrong, Doreen? he says. Why do you look so nervous?

I'm not, I say, which is a pretty stupid thing to say, seeing that he can probably hear my heart beat.

You're really special, Doreen, he says, and then he totally lays off me and turns around, like he doesn't care.

So I turn around to go back into my room because he's sort of freaking me out, and he grabs my arm and I snap back real quick because I'm not expecting it.

You're a really special girl, he says, like he's a zombie. Night of the living Matthews.

Uh, thanks, I say, all squirmy like a wet fish.

Alright, go now, he says, throwing my arm back at me. Go to bed, Doreen, you're grounded, you don't want to get in trouble.

He doesn't even look at me and he turns to go out the door and I practically run to my room and shut the door tight and put the chair from my desk up against it, under the doorknob. Then I stay awake for a long time, listening for noises.

The next morning, it's kind of late I guess, and there's this loud knock on my door.

Doreen, Dad says, Doreen, it's time to get up.

I twist around on my sheetless bed, and it actually feels kind of nice—the padded mattress with the plastic stitches. It's actually more comfortable than anyone would think.

Doreen, open the door.

I'm coming, I say, all annoyed.

Dad's always afraid to open my or Tracey's door because he's afraid he'll see us naked. Sometimes I think he must've covered his eyes when we were born because he didn't want to see us naked. This is why I think my parents probably never have sex. Well, I mean, they're both totally gross for one thing, and Mom's a nut, but I bet Dad never looks at her. I bet he doesn't even look in the mirror if he doesn't have to. Unless he's shaving or something.

I open the door, and he's standing there, looking down, hardly at me.

Doreen, the garage is filthy. You should have had it cleaned already, he says. Now you have plenty of time to do it. Are you listening to me?

Yes.

Take a shower, get dressed, and clean the garage. You are not to leave this house, he says.

He's looking at me.

You are not to talk on the phone to anyone.

But Ted— I say.

Not even Ted. You are grounded.

I want to tell him that Ted got all beat up and I have to do something. Somebody has to do something. That's what I think adults don't get. Somehow, when you get *older,* you let people do shitty things and you don't care. Or worse, you do care, and you just don't do anything about it. You turn into a slug. I mean, I guess I'm a slug too, but at least I'm trying not to be. And I'm only fourteen, not fifty-whatever.

Dad, look, I really have to talk to Ted, I say, which is a stupid thing to say, because now that Dad knows I want something, he's going to be all jazzed because he can take it away.

You should have thought of that before, he says, all self-righteous.

Then he turns to leave, but before he does, he says, I never thought you could be so irresponsible, and then he leaves.

I think to myself, Well, Hal, you should've thought of that before you had kids. But I do what he says anyway.

Except the shower part.

• • •

I'm sitting down in the garage, flipping playing cards from a deck across the floor.

Every time I close my eyes I see Matthew. I see him on top of me, moving back and forth. I can feel his stomach against mine. I see his eyes closed when mine weren't. The corners of his mouth were all curled up like a fish. I didn't move at all. Doreen Doreen Doreen. You're so beautiful.

My whole body shudders like I'm going to throw up. But I don't. And then last night. Maybe he's on drugs. That would explain a lot. I'm still sore. It would really sting if I took a shower.

I don't know why it's so important to Dad that I take a shower. I mean, I'm not stinking up the house or anything, and seeing that I'm not going anywhere in the outside world anytime soon, it's not like I'm going to *offend* anyone. Goddamn stupid Dad.

He can just eat a bunch of shit for all I care. My earliest memory of anything, I think, is of me being in the bathtub—I must've been three or four or something, and I was crying for some reason. I guess kids just cry about nothing at that age. But I was supposed to go to bed, I think, and I didn't want to, so I was throwing a fit, basically. And I just remember Dad coming in all pissed off and lifting me out of the tub by my armpits, like I was a dog or something. And I was still howling and crying and yelling and I'm sure there was baby snot everywhere—I swear, I don't think I'll ever have kids just so I won't have to deal with the baby snot. That is just too foul. And he didn't even towel me off. He just yanked this frilly nightgown over me, and I remember it sticking to me all over, and then he took me by the wrist and pulled me to my room and put me in bed, and then he turned off the lights and left. I remember shivering and crying still and my hair was wet against the pillow and I was lying there, all wet. I was supposed to go to sleep, I guess.

Good parenting, Dad. Bill Cosby's got nothing on you. You kicked one kid out because you couldn't handle him, one kid's a stupid slutty bitch, and the other's an outcast who doesn't bathe and who everybody hates.

That last one would be me.

The same books. The same fabric. The same stupid letters and papers and dust. Neat little piles. I find the box where I found Henry's postcard, but I don't even want to think about the dumb card anymore. It was pretty stupid of me to think I could find him in Chicago. There's no reason he'd stay there. He can do anything he wants. He could be climbing mountains somewhere. He could be in Africa for all I know. Or Burma or some place like that.

I pick the playing cards up off the floor and my stubby fingernails scrape the concrete. One chips but doesn't bleed, and I don't care anyway.

as loud as hell a ringing bell,
behind my smile it shakes my teeth.

Goddamn, now that song's going to be in my head all day. But I mean, I'd rather have Pixies running through my head than any grunge shit. It seems kind of dumb—all these words to songs I don't like are in my head. I mean, there could be something really good in my head instead. I could have the cure for cancer in there. Well, maybe not that, but something cool could be in there. Something cooler than "Oh What a Night." The translation to "Oh My Golly" maybe. A way to kill Alex Matten and his ohsotight princess and their stupid lizard friends.

I stack the playing cards in a neat little pile in my hand, and then I reach into my back pocket and pull out this book of matches that Ted handed to me at some point last night and never took back. 7-Eleven matches. I take them out and light one and let it burn down to my fingers until it hurts too much. Then I burn another. And another. I love matches so fucking much. Who knows why. I like matches more than the cigarettes, actually. That's so *dumb*. I'm so stupid sometimes.

I take the top card off the deck, and it's a seven of hearts, and I remember Tracey and her friends—maybe they were in junior high or something, and I tried to go into her room, where she and the rest of them were talking about hair and boys and whatever, and they had some deck of cards in front of them, telling each other's fortunes. Something like sevens meant distance, eights meant time, whatever. If you turned up a seven, it meant that you were separated from whatever boy because of distance. Whatever. I think they were all separated from boys because they were fucking *dorks*. Just show a little thigh, girls. Just put out and watch those sevens and eights disappear.

So I hold the seven of hearts in front of me by the edge, and I take out a match and strike it and light the card right up. It doesn't catch easily, I think because it's so slick and waxy. But then it does. First the edges catch and start curling, and it smells pretty nasty, and it keeps curling and I watch all those little hearts char. Barbecued hearts for dinner, kids.

Then this weird goo dribbles off the side a little and onto my hand, and it's hot as hell and I yelp and drop the card into a box. And it starts a thin line of smoke as the card burns and catches like crazy onto some old letters. It's a strange thing about me—I know that's wrong—that fire shouldn't be happening, that it can kill you, but it just looks so damn good to me right now. And I imagine each little heart is someone new—Alex Matten, Alexandra Stuart, Dave, Peter, Tracey, Mom, Dad. Sorry, guys. I'm really sorry I've burned you all beyond recognition.

Then I sort of snap out of it because the smoke goes up my nose and makes me cough a little, and I stand up and start stomping on the letters in the box until I'm pretty sure it's all out. Then I put the black ones at the bottom of the box. I'm not too worried because I'm the only one who's been in here in like, twenty years.

I open the little window and the door to air the place out, and I breathe in deep, and it makes me really want a cigarette.

I'm in my room, and it's nighttime now, and I've only been out to go to the bathroom. I'm surprised they don't carve a hatch in my door and slide bread and water through it. Mom and Dad have been out all day "doing errands." It makes me wonder how many errands people can have to do. Mom goes out and "does errands" every day of her life, and it's not like she comes back with all this stuff or anything. She usually comes back with nothing, or like, one bag. And then the next day she goes out to do more of these mystery errands.

I guess they're home now, but I don't feel like seeing them. I called Ted about twenty times when Mom and Dad were out, and he hasn't been home all day. I know I'm not supposed to even use the phone, but they can't put a goddamn padlock on the receiver or anything. I should've just gone over to Ted's when I had the chance, but I didn't know when Mom and Dad were coming home, and if they came home and I wasn't there, I would be so dead.

I'm thinking maybe I'll sneak out tonight.

I hear the phone ring, and I run for it, and sure enough, Mom and Dad are there, and Dad doesn't even look at me and picks up the phone.

Doreen's not allowed to use the phone, Ted. I'm sorry.

The hell you are, chief.

She'll call you when she's no longer grounded.

Dad says it so weird, like I'll call him when I'm no longer sleeping—as if it's something I'm doing. I can just hear Ted on the other line, pretending he doesn't know I'm grounded. Oh, OK, Mr. Severna, well yeah um I'll call back um some other time.

He hangs up the phone and looks at me.

Did you finish cleaning the garage?

I started, I say.

He nods and then he sits down and starts reading the newspaper.

I go into the kitchen where Mom is, and she's got rubber yellow gloves on, and she's scouring the toaster oven, and it's making this really horrible scratching sound. She is really into cleaning that toaster oven. She's sort of hunched over scrubbing and scrubbing, as if she's going to die if she doesn't get that thing spotless. I look at her face, and she's squinting her eyes, almost like Ted does when he can't see, which is all the time, and she's examining the toaster oven.

She's cleaning that toaster oven like she's trying to save its life. She loves that toaster oven. She needs that toaster oven.

I don't say anything to her and just go back in my room to listen to music and I just hope to God and Jesus and the devil please please please please don't let me end up like her.

I'm not going to lie about it—I'm getting really sick of this Anne Frank bullshit. If I don't get out of here and go to Ted's soon, I'm going to explode. I've listened to *Bossanova, Doolittle, Surfer Rosa, Come On, Pilgrim,* and the song "Manta Ray" about six thousand times.

My Manta Ray's alright,
My Manta Ray's alright . . .

I know your Manta Ray's alright. I'm sure it's great. I'm sure it's doing just fine. I don't even know what a manta ray even is, so I look it up in this dictionary I brought in from the garage. It only says, MANTA—A GIANT *RAY* WITH WINGLIKE PECTORAL FINS. ALSO MANTA RAY. Well, that really helps. So I look up Ray. It says, RAY—A CARTI-LAGINOUS FISH WITH A BROAD FLAT BODY, WIDELY EXPANDED FINS ON BOTH SIDES, AND A WHIPLIKE TAIL.

Great. What's the point of looking up a word if you just have to keep looking up like, a million more words. There's just no way I'm looking up cartilaginous.

And what the does that song mean anyway? His cartilaginous fish with winglike pectoral fins is alright? Whatever, man.

I really have to get out of here. I'm losing it.

• • •

After Mom and Dad go to their room for the night, I decide to call Ted, so I walk on my toes into the living room and grab the phone. But then, all of a sudden, I don't feel like calling Ted anymore. I just stand there for a second in the dark and hold the receiver and listen to the dial tone.

Cars drive down the street, and I watch the headlights shine into the dark living room and flash across the walls in moving streaks. And I still just stand there and listen to the dial tone. I start thinking about which way the cars are going, like north or south, or what, and I realize I don't really know any of that. I mean, I know that San Francisco is north, and that Chicago is east, and New York is even more east, but that's about all I can say.

Then I think, maybe New York.

I dial 411 and ask for New York information, and the lady says the area code's 212. I write on the little phone pad, 1-212-555-1212, and it looks like a fake number to me, but I dial it anyway, and when the lady asks, What city, I really don't know what to say. I really don't know what I'm doing.

Uh, New York City, I whisper.

What listing? she says, sounding annoyed.

All these operators are really abrupt. I know that's probably the name of the game if you're an operator, but it wouldn't kill them to be a little bit nice, especially because it's obvious I'm young and don't go around making long distance phone calls every day. And this lady's even worse than the others. At least Maude told me her name.

Last name's Severna, I say, sounding out the word slow.

I hear her typing, and then I say, First name's Henry.

Clack clack clack.

No Severna, she says.

I start scratching at the edge of the phone stand with my fingertip and get an idea.

Well, is there, um, any name that, you know, sounds close to that?

She sighs like I just asked her the toughest question, like I just asked her about physics.

Ma'am, she says, all impatient. There's too many here—Severn, Severns, Severo, Severso—

She keeps rattling names off, and I grind my teeth a little, and feel my heart start pounding hard. And then I hear a car pull into the driveway, see the lights flash in the living room.

OK, thanks, I say, and I hang up quickly.

I think it's probably Tracey and Matthew.

I go into the kitchen to pretend to get a glass of soda, and I hear them come in.

It's just so unfair, Tracey's saying.

For some reason, I don't think she's talking about world hunger. I'm sure The Body Shop ran out of her favorite lip gloss, or she can't get any more stupid platform sneakers because she already has them all.

Then they come into the kitchen, and Matthew looks all tired and gray and maybe like he's going to throw up, and Tracey doesn't look too good either. I mean, she always looks *dumb,* but she looks tired too, and really extra thin. I guess I kind of surprise her, because she sort of jumps when she sees me.

Jesus, Dor, she says. Don't fucking lurk around like that.

Matthew doesn't look at me.

What's up with you looking like hell? she says to me. When's the last time you washed your fucking hair?

I shrug.

I stand across from Matthew, and he looks at me finally, his eyes all heavy, and I remember him leaning against me last night, and I start to feel like how he looks. All gray and tired and like I'm going to collapse. He's staring at me now. It's like he's *making* me tired. I'm beginning to wonder if he ever goes home.

All this time, Tracey's rooting around in the refrigerator like a groundhog.

Where's the fucking white grape juice? she says to me.

I don't fucking know where the fucking white grape juice is, I say to her.

God, could you be any more annoying? Tracey says, still looking in the refrigerator.

There's soda in there, I say, and it doesn't really sound like my voice even.

I just let Matthew stare me down.

Tracey slams the refrigerator door shut and says, I don't drink soda.

Of course she doesn't, I think. She doesn't drink soda and doesn't eat chocolate because it's *fattening* and doesn't eat meat because she's got to save the animals even though she treats people like *shit* and doesn't like to smell like anything except perfume and makeup and doesn't like anything *icky* and doesn't like to break a sweat.

She probably has a cool towel over her head when she and Matthew do it.

I'm just trying to help, I say.

Tracey exhales, all annoyed.

Aren't you grounded? Shouldn't you be in your room, playing with yourself? she snaps back at me.

I feel my ears get hot and I look away from Matthew and at Tracey laughing and I grip my glass so hard I think it's going to break.

Tracey? I say, really quietly.

She looks up at me with her beady rat eyes ready to roll, thinking Doreen's such an idiot such a dork such a baby.

You are such *a fucking girl!* I scream, and I throw all the soda in my glass at her.

Now we're standing across from each other, cola's dripping off her face and her hair and her baby T and her mouth's open, shocked as hell. And so am I, kind of.

I look at Matthew, and he starts laughing.

Tracey's just holding her arms out, looking at herself like Carrie after she gets pig's blood dumped on her at the prom. You little bitch, she squeals, and she lunges for me, to grab me or slap me or something, but I just run for my room, and I hear her screaming at Matthew.

It's not funny, you asshole!

I slam the door and lock it and squat down on the other side of it, and then I hear Mom and Dad come out of their room, and they're all squawking like birds.

What happened? Mom says.

She dumped soda on me! Tracey whines, almost crying, and it's all so fucking funny I just have to laugh.

Doreen, come out here right now and apologize to your sister, Dad says, banging his fist on my door.

No way, I shout through.

I hear Tracey crying and bitching to Mom, and Dad keeps banging on the door.

Doreen Jane Severna, you have screwed up one too many times— *Get out here now!* he screams, and it makes me shudder.

I open the door and stare at them all. Tracey's still all wet, Mom's in her weird frilly nightie, Dad's in sweatpants and a T-shirt and his face is all red. It is kind of scary when he gets this angry. Matthew's not there. I guess he went in Tracey's room.

Apologize to your sister, Dad says, slow and mechanical.

I'm *really* sorry, Tracey, I say, all sarcastic, and I know it won't fly with Dad, but I just can't help myself.

You better drop that tone of voice right now. Right now, Dad says, all in my face.

When parents say that, all you have to do is say it quieter, and they automatically think you mean it. I mean, really, how can you not mean something, and then totally mean it a second later? And Dad wouldn't know if I meant it or not. He's not a psychic friend.

I'm really sorry, Tracey, I say, looking at my feet.

Then I just leave them out there, and I go back into my room and start giggling so hard I have to stick my face in the pillow.

• • •

I figure I'll go call Ted, because Mom and Dad are probably asleep by now, and I guess so are Tracey and Matthew. I open my door real quietly and sneak into the living room, and I'm kind of paranoid and really awake. I'm all charged up. I pick up the phone and sit on the floor, and I dial Ted.

Hello.

It's me, I whisper.

What the hell did you do? he says, and I start smiling when I hear his voice and who knows why that is. He says, Are you, like, grounded until you die?

Or until they die, I say.

God, it's like *Flowers in the Attic,* he says. And then he starts saying, Eat the cookie, mother, eat the cookie, in this really shrill voice like the chick in that movie, and it almost makes me wet myself.

Shut up, shut up, I say, trying so hard not to laugh out loud that I think I'm going to fart or throw up or something.

Can you get out?

I think so. I have to wait a few more minutes, though. To make sure they're asleep.

OK, he says. Just be sure to . . .

And then he trails off.

Just be sure to what? I say.

I hear him inhaling really loud, and he says, Just be sure to . . . *Eat the cookie, Mother*!

I sort of choke because I'm laughing so hard and so quietly and I say, You're such a fucker, and I hang up.

Then I look at the front door and I think maybe I can leave through there, but I'm sure Dad would hear my keys in the door when I came back in. And anyway, I can just go through the window again. Now I sort of know how.

I start to go back to my room and I'm having such a goddamn hard time trying not to laugh, I practically have to cover my mouth. What is it with me? Since when am I so giggly? Sometimes, Ted can put me in this kind of mood for no good reason.

It's so weird—I haven't talked to or seen Ted in twenty-four hours—that's all, and it feels like I haven't seen him in about ten years. It's like I *have* to see him. Like if I don't, I just won't make it. Maybe it's because he makes me laugh so hard. Which is weird, because when I'm with him lately, I get angry because he's such a dork. I'm just all confused.

I go back to my room, but before I go in, I hear noises from Tracey's room. Sex noises. Tracey's grunting like a piglet, and Matthew's not really making any sounds at all, I don't think. I can hear the bed. I don't want to close my eyes because I think I'll see Matthew's face above me, moving up and down over me. I just stand there, in front of the door, and I don't really realize I'm shaking or that I'm getting chills all over.

He's on top of her. Right now.

I stare at her door, and I think what would happen if I opened it. I could go in and stand there and watch them. Watch Tracey's gross face underneath him. Watch him moving up and down and maybe covering her eyes too. I could just stand there. Maybe I could bend down so I'd be right by their faces, and I could stare at them until they noticed. Tracey would probably scream and then Mom and Dad would come in and see that they were doing it, and that would be pretty cool, but I don't think I want to see it at all.

I look down at my hands, and I remember Mom taking my hands and, this wasn't too long ago, a couple of years ago maybe, and she said, Your hands look so young and smooth. Look at mine.

So I did look at hers, and they were all wrinkly and kind of bony, and I remember thinking that was a weird thing for her to say, but she's always full of weird things to say. I also kind of liked that she said that to me.

For some reason, I'm crying now, and I can still hear sick sounds from Tracey's room, and I go into my room and put my shoes on and head for the window.

Wow, Ted says at the door. You look like shit.

You should talk, I say, and we go down to the basement. His black eye and bruises haven't exactly healed, and he's so skinny and sick-looking anyway.

Where the hell have you been all day? I say. I called about a thousand times.

I had to run errands with my mom, he says.

Everyone's all about running errands around here.

What did you tell her about your face? I ask.

I told her you've been beating me.

Are you serious?

No, dork-ass, he says. I told her I got in a fight.

Did she freak out?

For a while. Then she spent some quality time with Jack Daniels, and it was all OK.

And then you ran errands? I say.

Yeah. Her driving when she's all fucked-up is pretty funny. She ran a red in Old Town.

Shit. Did anyone see?

Well, I'm sure somebody saw, but no cops, anyway. I just said to her, Mom, that was so red.

We both laugh. I can totally see Ted's mom wearing her big-ass sunglasses that make her look like a fly, driving with one hand on the wheel and the other hanging out the window, holding her Benson and Hedges far enough away so it doesn't catch on all the hair spray on her head.

Shit, I forgot to tell you. Listen to this, I say, and Ted perks up.

I don't know why the both of us are so happy and excited right now. I mean, both our lives *suck,* so it doesn't really make a whole lot of sense that we're sitting here, hashing over all the shitty things that are going on and laughing while we do it. I guess we don't have much of a choice, though.

I tell him the story about throwing soda on Tracey, and he gulps up every word and his mouth's hanging open by the end.

For Christ's *ass,* Dor, you are so cool! he says, and then he leans over to hug me or something, which is a little weird, and we both know it, so he backs off.

I can't believe it, he says, shaking his head. What did her boyfriend do?

Huh? I say, not knowing for a second who the hell he's talking about.

You know, what's-his-lips, Michael? Ted says, not remembering his name.

Matthew, I say.

Yeah—what did he do?

What I almost say is, He fucked me, Ted, and I really didn't have anything to do with it, and I thought I wanted him to, but it hurt really bad and he didn't ask if he could, he just started and I was just lying there letting him but I still want him to look at me but I don't think I want him to fuck me any more but he said I was beautiful and perfect and everything and why don't you just get it, Ted, because if you knew, if you really knew, you'd get it.

He just started laughing, I say.

Really? Ted says, all excited. That's so cool. Maybe he's not such a scab.

Ted?

What?

Nothing, I say.

I really was about to tell him, I swear.

Later, when I figure I better get home, Ted and I suddenly don't have anything to say.

Do you think you can get out tomorrow night? he says.

I don't know. I don't see why not, I say, kicking at the carpet with the toe of my foot.

The wind blows bad outside, and the whole house feels like it's shifting for a second.

Ted sits up and kind of jumps. He looks scared and his eyes are all wide, looking all around, even though there are no windows in his basement.

You think it's them, don't you? I say.

No, Ted says, all annoyed.

But I know he does. I know he probably can't stop thinking about it. When someone does something like that to you, it's just all over your head no matter what you do, and it will be until you do something. That's what I've tried to tell Ted before. That's what I've tried to tell everyone.

We'll get them, Ted, I say. I'm still thinking of the perfect way.

Yeah, yeah, Ted says. We'll "get" them, Dor, and then they'll get us and we'll get them, and we'll all just keep getting each other until we die. That's real good, he says, all sarcastic.

Well, it won't be any good when you think like that, I say.

Dor, Ted says, all annoyed and fakely grown-up. I don't want to do anything. I don't care enough.

I don't believe you.

He laughs.

Well, what then? What's your master plan, chief? What are you thinking we can do that'll get them so good they'll never bother us again?

Truth is, I don't know. I keep kicking at the carpet because it's peeling up in so many places it's barely even a carpet. It's like a bunch of throw rugs, but the shag's so worn down, it's more like someone cut up a bunch of wigs and put them on the floor.

We could burn their fucking houses down, I say.

Ted laughs and says, OK, Dor, let's go to *jail* because people are mean to us.

It's not just them, I say.

Who else are you talking about?

Everyone. Just . . . everyone, I say, pacing. The world.

So what are you going to do, Doreen? Burn down the whole world?

I don't look at him and just keep kicking the carpet and say real quietly, Yeah.

The next morning is bad. I wake up to Dad knocking again.

Doreen, it's time to get up, he's saying, all stern.

I feel all barfy because I got home at like, four or something. So I get up and wipe the crud out of my eyes and stumble to the door and open it. Dad looks away, I guess because I'm in my T-shirt and underwear.

What time is it? I say.

It's nine.

Dad, I'm really tired, I say. I need to sleep for a little while longer.

You've slept for a good ten hours, at least, he says. That's enough for anyone.

I don't argue and I put jeans and shoes on and I'm so tired I think I'm going to die, and I go into the kitchen, and Mom is wiping down the kitchen table, even though nobody's had breakfast yet.

Hi, I say.

Mom looks up like her head's weighted down with rocks and says, Good morning, Doreen.

Come on, Doreen, Dad says, and I follow him out to the garage, and he opens the door to it and we both just stand there.

Well? he says.

What? I say, not really knowing what he's asking.

He looks at me like I'm crazy and says, This place is an absolute sty. What have you been doing in here?

I shrug.

I'm just . . . organizing stuff, I say.

Listen to me, Doreen, he says, You'd better get your act together soon. No more outbursts, no more talking back.

He keeps talking and I partially tune out because I know it's coming—the bit about how I live under his roof.

You have upset your mother over and over again, and I'm sick of it. I am tired of your behavior. It's the last thing I need. You are screwing up way too much, and as long as you live in my house, you have to do what I tell you to do.

Go, Dad, I think, you are now no longer a real human, but a total stereotype. Good going. You're having a *smashing* week.

Do you understand me?

I don't say anything.

Answer me.

Fine, he says, and he turns around to leave. Before he does, though, he stops and says, This place better be clean by tonight.

Then he leaves.

Or what? Or you'll double-ground me? You'll take away my bathroom privileges? He's always got to do that too, he's always got to say one last thing before he makes his grand exit. So dramatic. At least he didn't find out about the little fire, though. Although, at this point, everybody hates me so much and they all probably think I'm such a headcase that it wouldn't even matter. Doreen's foulmouthed, dirty, rude, crazy, stupid, and oh yes, in her spare time, she enjoys setting fires. I mean, who cares.

So again with the books and the fabrics and papers. I figure I'll probably just make it look all organized, but I'm not sifting through all this stuff again. I'll just stack things. One on top of the other. Neat little piles.

I start thinking about Matthew, but it really is making me feel gross to think about him so I try to stop. For a second I wonder if I should tell Ted. I almost did last night. I start getting angry again because Ted doesn't even care about getting the Alexes. I don't understand him sometimes.

They beat him down, inside and out, because they can, because it makes them feel cool, because they have *nothing* else to do, and he just takes it. He just lies there and takes it.

He just lies there. He just lies there.

I stop stacking.

I stop stacking because it seems like I can't do anything. And I start crying again. I'm all about crying lately. What is it with me? And I'm so sweaty and dirty all the time. I wipe some grease off my forehead and look at it, all shiny on my hand mixed in with my tears. Salt and water. That's all I'm made of practically. I can't stop crying so I curl up in a little ball and close my eyes and grunt and whimper and I think I could die, and I think what if I did die, right here, right now. I feel like I've been awake for a thousand hours and without even thinking about it, I fall asleep on the cement floor, and I'm so tired that it feels pretty goddamn comfortable.

I have dreams of being in Ted's house, except it's not really his house, it's like bizarro Ted's house, and me and him are in the bizarro basement, and he's telling me how we can't go upstairs because there's ice all over the floor, like a hockey rink. But for some reason, we have to get out of the house. If we don't, something really bad will happen to us. I tell Ted we're going to have to try to get out by going upstairs, and he says no we can't, Doreen, we can't, and he starts crying like crazy and screaming and holding onto me, saying you can't go up there, Doreen. I shake him off me, and I go upstairs, and it's all crazy like a maze and Ted's mom is on the ice floor, passed out, drooling. I start to walk across it and it burns bad so I start running and then I guess I realize it's not ice but glass, and shards of it are stuck in my feet and it hurts like hell. And I pull them out, one by one, each piece of glass out of my feet, and my feet look like steaks or something, all bloody and meaty, like something that should be hanging on a hook in a window.

When I wake up, I'm shaking, and it's so quiet, I'm almost scared. I look down at my feet, just to check, which is stupid, I know. I mean, I know there wasn't really any glass in my feet—where would it have come from?—but it felt so goddamn real. I swear I could feel them, like ice picks in my feet, and I could feel them slicing me open as I pulled them out.

And then I get up off the floor and I leave the garage, and I start walking.

• • •

I end up in front of Ted's house, and I rap at the back door, and there's no answer. I even go around to the front door and ring the bell, and there's still no answer, and then I just stand in front of his house.

There is so much oil on my face that when I sweat I taste it. You could fry *chicken* on my face. I kind of like it, though. Ted said that once, if you're dirty, nobody'll fuck with you. He was just being stupid, trying to act all tough, but maybe he's right.

I shouldn't be here. I'm grounded. I shouldn't be anywhere. I shouldn't be at home and I shouldn't be at Ted's and I shouldn't be with Matthew and I really shouldn't be thinking all this crazy shit all the time.

I think for a second, I should just try real hard to be normal and get along with *someone* besides Ted, but I've really tried before, and there doesn't seem to be much use after a while. After a while, trying gets so old. Ted's house is empty, and there's no one on the street. It's hot. It's like the desert out here. I wait awhile for Ted to come home, but he doesn't, and I feel sort of like an idiot just standing in the middle of the street in front of his house, but I really don't feel like sitting on his front steps or the curb.

I finally just turn around and walk back home. I know that if Dad checked on me in the garage and found out I wasn't there, he'll probably send me away to military school, but I just can't try to care anymore. Everything's such an effort, even caring a little. Even being such a gigantic fuck-up wears me out.

• • •

It is so quiet on the street that I think, for a minute, maybe there's been some kind of nuclear war and I'm the only one left. It wouldn't be so bad, I guess. I get back to my house, and Mom and Dad's car is there. So is Matthew's. The door to the garage is open. Oh well. Looks like I'm caught again.

I walk in through the front door, and Tracey and Matthew are sitting around. Matthew's reading a magazine and doesn't look up at me when I come in. Tracey's on the phone, and she looks up at me for a second.

Mom, Dad, Doreen's home! she screams, putting her hand over the receiver.

Yeah, that's right, sweetie, I think. Tell them. Tell on me—there's *nothing* else they can do to me for leaving Severna premises while grounded. Maybe they'll sue me. Maybe they'll chain me up in the garage. Maybe they'll just make me live here for four more years.

Mom and Dad come out—I guess they were in their room, and they both stare at me. There's been a lot of staring going on around here lately. Dad's angry, Mom's a crying mess. Alert the media.

Mom, can you make her take a shower? She smells like ass, Tracey says all snotty.

Watch your mouth, Tracey, Dad says, all calm and angry.

We stare some more. Me and Dad stare actually. I don't even look at Mom. I'm tired of looking at Mom and worrying I'll make her have a breakdown. She has breakdowns over expired coupons.

I went to Ted's, I say, not sorry at all, and I wait for them to lay into me, to tell me how now I've just gone too far by leaving. They're going to make it sound like I've jumped bail and took off for Mexico.

But they don't. They don't say anything, and then I hear Mom exhale all loudly, and she says in this really quiet shaky voice,

Doreen, you shouldn't have thrown away your sheets just because you have your period, she says, like it's a line she's been reading off a page, like it's a line she's been practicing for awhile.

Oh God, Tracey says, all annoyed and embarrassed because Mom's talking about periods in front of Matthew.

Without thinking, I say, all annoyed, I don't have my goddamn period.

Then I realize.

Tracey hangs up the phone.

I feel Matthew's eyes on me, but I don't look at him, and my heart starts to pound.

It pounds so loud in my ears and all over me. I can feel the blood in my head. I feel like throwing up. I feel like lying down. Over and over again in my head, I'm thinking What is happening what is happening what is happening.

Mom and Dad stare some more. I hear Mom start crying. Dad's face looks like it's made out of metal—all angles.

Wait, just wait, Tracey says, like she can't believe it. Let me get this straight. You and Ted did it in your bed?

Tracey! Dad yells. Shut your mouth.

I shake my head no and open my mouth to talk but I can't. I just see Dad staring at me, looking angry and sad too, I guess. He almost shakes his head with me. It looks to me like he's thinking, How could you, Doreen. How could you screw up like this.

I . . . I, Mom says, crying, I have to . . . I have to, she just keeps saying, talking all crazy like some whacked-out bag lady, I have to do . . .

And she goes over to the kitchen counter and starts looking around for something she has to do. She's just mumbling to herself over there, and I can hear Tracey snickering, but it's like there's this tunnel between me and Dad, and I can't look anywhere else except at him. Not even at Matthew.

She thought she could hide it by dumping the sheets, I hear Tracey say to Matthew.

There was blood on your mattress, Dad says to me. Your mother was worried.

My heart is so loud and it is so hot in here all the time and I think, what were they doing in my room, they must have checked the garage and I wasn't there, and then they came in there and I guess they saw—my mind is going crazy. I think I am going crazy. And they think it was Ted.

I think I should call Ted's mother, Dad says. And I don't want you to see him.

I think of poor little Ted with all his bruises and how he can't skate, and how everyone beats him up all the time. And I think how I won't get to see him again for a long time, probably never.

I see Tracey get up and say quietly to Matthew, I'm really sorry you had to see all this . . . this is really embarrassing blah blah blah, and Matthew nods, and they start to head for the door.

Is this true, Doreen? Dad asks, as if he doesn't already think I did, as if whatever I say makes a difference to him, as if whatever I say makes a difference to anyone.

I look over at Matthew and he looks over at me for a second and shrugs and smiles like he's saying, Oh well Doreen, it's your fault. You're not really all that perfect. It looks like he's saying, It's not my fault. I didn't do anything. It's a better-luck-next-time smile.

It, I say, my mouth feeling like it's full of cotton balls, and I see Tracey and Matthew leaving, and all of a sudden, I think that if I say this thing right this second, right now, maybe something will change. Maybe one thing will be alright. Just one skinny little thing.

It wasn't Ted, I say.

That sure gets everyone's attention. Mom turns around from the counter she's about to wax and polish, and Tracey turns around from the door, because she really wants to hear this, and she has no idea what's coming.

Matthew stops in his tracks, and he's still turned around, with his back to me, and he won't look at me. I'll *make* you look at me.

I look at all of them once more because I have a feeling like we're all going to explode or just disappear or the house will fall down any minute.

It was Matthew, I say.

The whole room stops for a second, and I close my eyes and feel puke rising in my throat, and I really am expecting this place to explode or catch fire or something, but when I open my eyes, everyone's still standing right where they were before.

Yeah, right, Tracey says, still laughing. Dad, she has just gone too far. Look at what a freak she is, Tracey starts saying.

Will you stop *lying?* Mom sobs, and she practically collapses against the counter.

And I can't do anything anymore. I don't even know what I could say to anyone right now. Not even Ted. Not even Henry. I sort of crumple down to my knees and start crying for the millionth time today but I can't help it. I can't help anything.

Now she's making up trash about Matthew, Tracey's saying. What is up with that? This is just so unfair.

I look up to see Dad coming toward me. He's standing right in front of me, and I think he's going to yank me up by my hair or something, and I don't even care if he does. He could shave my fucking head right now and I wouldn't care.

Matthew? I hear Dad say, as if he's going to ask him, as if he believes me.

But he doesn't really finish the question.

I turn to look at Matthew, who's standing there looking nervous, but not in the way he should. He looks nervous like he's just some next-door neighbor who's walked in on a little family squabble.

I'm sorry, Mr. Severna, Matthew says, clearing his throat, but I think Doreen might have a little crush on me.

He keeps talking, saying something else, explaining why I would make up this crazy thing and how it's natural for a girl my age to have these kinds of crushes and how he would never do that, and I'm just a mess on the floor, and I'm rocking back and forth and hugging my knees to my chest now.

Matthew, Dad says again, and this time he gets down where I am and real quietly, gently almost, he says to me, Stand up for me, Doreen.

He doesn't yank me. He puts one arm around me and holds me up and pulls me up to my feet, and I'm still shaking and crying. Dad stands behind me, still holding me, and then he lets go real gently and starts walking toward Matthew and Tracey.

Matthew, Dad says, getting up real close to him. Matthew, did you do this to my little girl? he says in the robot voice, and I can't see much through the blur of my crying, but I do see that Matthew looks like he's about to pee.

No, sir, Matthew says.

Dad, stop it. This is crazy, Tracey whines.

Dad just holds one finger up to Tracey, and I swear, there must be electricity or fire or something in that finger because Tracey, for once, stops yammering.

I am going to ask you again, Dad says. Did you do this to my little girl?

I sort of stop blubbering for a second. I can't see Dad's face, but Matthew's facing me and he doesn't look all that comfortable. Dad can be pretty scary when he wants to be. And he believes me. He believes me.

Matthew opens his mouth to answer but doesn't, and he actually looks at me and all of a sudden, I feel like I got something back. I stare at him. Out of all the times I've stared at people, the people I can't stare down are Matthew and Dad. I bet Matthew's never met anyone who can stare him down, and now he's got the one person who can beat him right in his face and he doesn't know what to do.

Matthew doesn't answer.

Matthew, what the fuck? Tracey says, still not getting it because she's a fucking idiot.

No one says anything for a second. Or maybe they do. My legs feel like sticks or like they're made of sand and could just snap any time now. I gulp down some snot and salt and bite my bottom lip and watch.

Dad, this is *crazy,* Tracey says, Matthew didn't do anything to Doreen!

But Dad's not even looking at Tracey. Dad doesn't want to hear it from Tracey. He keeps looking at Matthew, and Tracey's holding onto Matthew's arm, almost trying to drag him out of here, and Matthew still looks all nervous, and I kind of enjoy that.

Why are you so nervous, Matthew? Dad says, all sarcastic, and I almost want to cheer, do the wave, something.

Sir, Matthew squeaks out. Sir, I would never touch Doreen.

Dad turns around to look at me.

Doreen, he says quietly, his forehead all crumpled up, and I realize, he wants my opinion.

He's asking me what he should do.

Dad, I say, and then I feel my voice get all crackly like it does before I start crying, and I whisper, Look at me.

Dad does look at me, and I can't be looking too pretty. My hair's so greasy and matted, it's like one plastic piece, like a helmet on a stormtrooper. My fingernails are bitten down to the bone and I'm so, so dirty and smelly and oily and zitty. I look like a pile of shit, and he's got to know. He's got to.

Tracey starts yammering again. Dad, we're leaving, this is such bullshit, you should ground that little idiot *forever.* She did it with Ted and she's trying to blame Matthew. She . . . she . . .

And then she turns back around to Matthew, and I see him nodding, and Dad says, Tracey, shut your mouth and get your mother a glass of water.

But, Dad—

Tracey! he yells. Get your mother a goddamn glass of water!

Tracey looks all confused and starts to back away from Dad, and Matthew's up against the door, and after Dad clocks him good one time, everything just happens so fast.

From what I remember, Mom was crying and wailing, Tracey was screeching and tried to stop Dad before he hit Matthew again. Matthew was all curled up on the floor and I think maybe he tried to hit Dad, but I didn't see too well because I just wanted to get Tracey off Dad so I yanked her off him with everything I have in me and then we fell on the floor, and Mom was screaming, Stop it! Stop it! and being all hysterical. And I was holding Tracey by the wrists, sitting on top of her, and she wriggled one hand free and scratched her rat nails deep into my neck, from right below my chin almost down to my chest. And then I just remember staring into her stupid face and she was yelling at me, You stupid *liar* and I just hit her—not with an open hand either, but with a balled-up fist. I felt pretty cool about that because she started crying and bleeding and I started yelling at her, You're so fucking stupid, and I started hitting her more and more, grabbing at her hair and skin, and she was grabbing at me, and then Dad just picked me up off her, and I was all arms and legs, kicking and batting the air, looking like a giant spider, and Matthew was still on the floor, and Mom went over to Tracey and everyone was screaming still, and Dad just lifted me out and opened the front door, and we left.

• • •

Get in the car, Doreen, he says.

Where are we going?

Get in the car.

So I do, and I'm shaking and crying still, and I can still hear Mom and Tracey howling.

I get in the car, and Dad pulls out his keys and turns it on, and Mom and Tracey, who looks all beat up, come running out, and Mom's screaming, Harry! Harry, what are you doing?!

But Dad doesn't even look at them. He just puts the car in reverse and takes off. I watch them through my blurry eyes, Tracey holding her bloody nose, screaming at me, calling me a bitch, and Mom crying, and Dad's not even looking. Dad doesn't seem to give half a shit.

We peel out, and then we just drive for a while without saying anything. I'm still crying because I can't seem to stop, and my neck's all bloody and gross, and I look over at Dad, and his mouth is bleeding a little. I guess Matthew did hit him back.

At a stoplight, Dad leans across me and opens the glove compartment and takes out some napkins that are in there and gives them to me. I try to give him one, and he holds up his hand, refusing it.

Dad, you're bleeding, I manage to say between choking sounds.

Dad looks all puzzled and so he leans up to look in the rearview mirror, and he sees the blood on his mouth, and he takes the napkin from my hand and wipes it. The two of us sit there, wiping dark blood off our faces, and I stop crying and just look out the window, and when the light turns green, Dad drives us to the freeway.

• • •

Now that I really look, I don't think I look too bad. Neither does Dad. I mean, Tracey really took a swipe at me, and she hit me a few times, and Matthew's not a small guy at all and he must've hit Dad a few times. But all Dad had was that little bit of blood by his mouth. Other than that, we're just sweaty and our hair's all messed up. I mean, it could be a lot worse.

Me and Dad: 2. Tracey and Matthew: 0. And Mom gets a 0 too, just for being such a freak. Maybe actually though, she gets a 1, because she should get more than Tracey and Matthew.

I start laughing because I don't know what the hell I'm thinking about. It's weird when you're really tired like I am—the nuttiest things sound so good, they sound like something you'd say any time.

Dad looks over at me while I laugh, and then he just stares back at the freeway, and since he doesn't tell me to stop laughing for no reason, I don't. And even if he did, I probably still wouldn't. I mean, I'm not telling him to stop driving.

Dad gets off the freeway in Hollywood, and we go down to Hollywood Boulevard, which is so glitzy and tacky, but I sort of like it for some reason. Even though I've never been to Las Vegas, I always think that it must kind of look like Hollywood Boulevard. We drive around Hollywood for a while, and I'm just liking staring out the window at everyone.

We go past the Virgin Megastore on Sunset, and I'm just aching to pull over and go in. I've been in there once, and it makes Tower look like a lemonade stand. There are, like, a thousand aisles and listening stations and when you look down at the first floor from the stairs going up to the movie section it looks like some crazy beautiful maze. It's pretty much like heaven except there are always all these assholes shopping there.

But we keep driving past it, and eventually we get on another freeway, and I think we might be going in a circle, and Dad's showing no sign that we're ever going to stop.

Dad, where are we going?

He shakes his head as he answers.

I don't know, Doreen.

We stop, though. In Pacific Palisades. On some random street. The people who live here are really rich. The houses are huge and really new-looking, like they were all just built last week, but they couldn't've been, because Pacific Palisades has been here awhile.

It's right near the water here. I can see it from where we're parked. There's some grassy area with benches, and then a cliff almost, and then ocean. It's really nice looking, except that I'm kind of afraid to swim in the ocean. Sharks, the tide—there's a lot to deal with.

I roll down the window and lean my head out there and try to smell the water, but I can't really. I do breathe in a bunch of pollen and flower smells from the grassy area, and I sneeze. I blow my nose into one of the napkins in my hands.

Bless you, Dad says.

Thanks.

When I sneeze, I usually never know whether or not I'm supposed to wait for someone to say Bless you, or if I'm just supposed to bust out with, Excuse me. That's one of those things that no one's ever told me about.

I look at Dad, and he's staring out, maybe not even at the water, really, just out there. I guess I haven't really thought about it before, but my father's really old. He's fifty-eight years old. Mom's so much younger than him. His hair is gray, and it's starting to get white, and his face has a lot of folds and wrinkles. He's still really strong, though. He still really did Matthew in, and he can pick me up without thinking about it. Matthew really didn't have a shot against Dad at all, actually. He was probably not too bad-looking when he was young.

How's your neck, he says to me all of a sudden.

I lean up to look in the mirror, and I'm not bleeding anymore, but there are huge welts where Tracey scratched me. I touch them lightly, and they sting and they're really puffy, like I've stuffed tissues under my skin.

It's fine, I say. How's your mouth?

Dad just nods, and I know that means it's fine. Dad always seems to choose nodding over speaking whenever he can.

I had to get out of there, he says to me.

I feel like saying he really doesn't have to explain to me how he had to get out of that house.

If I'd stayed, I would have killed that boy, he says, staring straight ahead.

I try to swallow some spit or something, but my mouth is so dry that I just kind of gulp air.

You did the right thing, Dad says to me.

What? I say, because I can't believe he's congratulating me on letting Matthew fuck me.

By telling me, he says.

Dad, I say, and I get all nervous because I think he might hate me if he knows I didn't fight, that I had thought about Matthew doing it a hundred times.

Dad, I sort of let him, I say.

Dad shakes his head this time and says, Doreen, as old as you think you think you are, you're not that old, and that makes all the difference between letting him and actually agreeing and wanting him to.

I look down.

I know that might be difficult for you to understand—

No, I say. No, I kind of get what you mean.

Dad nods.

There's something else I would like to talk to you about, he says.

I look up at him, because I really don't know what else is so serious besides what just happened, and then he reaches into his pocket for something and pulls out Henry's postcard which is all folded up, probably from being un-balled up and straightened and read when he and Mom were in my room.

I feel caught suddenly.

Dad puts the card on the dashboard in front of us. Did you find that in the garage? he asks.

I nod.

I haven't seen it in a long time, he says.

You've seen it before? I say, surprised.

Yes, I remember when it came in the mail.

I look at him, his voice and face aren't changing at all, staring out the window like he talks about this every day with me.

Henry was a very angry boy, he says, even though I didn't even ask. Then he closes his eyes and sort of tilts his head, as if he's going to go to sleep.

He was very cruel to your mother and I, he says. He was uncontrollable.

Why? I say, because I just can't help myself.

I don't know, Dad says, opening his eyes. We didn't know what to do. We tried to help him—we sent him to a doctor.

I picture Henry in a doctor's office, sitting in some big leather chair with some stupid shrink asking him about his dreams or something.

They wanted to put him in a home, where he could get help, where he wouldn't hurt anyone, but your mother insisted that we could take care of him, and we really believed we could, he says.

Dad looks so beaten down talking about this. I think, actually, just thinking about it is making him tired, making him get older by the second.

Why did you make him leave? I ask, sounding very small.

Dad turns to me.

I never made him leave, Doreen, he says. He left. He had threatened all of us, and I . . . I just couldn't have that.

What did he say? I say, starting to cry again.

He threatened to burn the house down, he threatened to kill your mother and I. He threatened to hurt you and Tracey.

I feel a rock in my throat.

And one night, I locked him in his room, because I didn't know what else to do, and the next morning he was gone, Dad says.

I look down and feel tears going down my face, and I see them drip onto my lap. All of a sudden, I can't see the picture of Henry too well in my head. All of a sudden he's not some dark strong boy, blowing smoke rings and being a smartass. He's this skinny little punk, pissed off at everything, pissed off at me, even. And I mean, what the hell could I have done to him to make him angry at me? I was only four.

Do you think about him? I say to Dad.

Dad almost smiles.

Every day, Doreen. Every single day.

I look out at the water and rub my eyes with the back of my hand, trying to stop crying but I can't. I think I'm just going to keep crying for the rest of my life.

He turns to me.

Why did you bring me here? I say, nodding to the ocean.

Dad shrugs and says, Sometimes you have to do things before you know why you're doing them.

I *know* it's a cheesy thing for him to say, but I kind of like it anyway, and we sit there and stare out for a little while longer, and then Dad starts the car and we stop for gas, and then we follow all those impossible fast freeways home.

I guess I fall asleep in the car, because when we get home, it's dark, and I don't really remember it getting dark. It seems like it was daytime a second ago. Dad pulls into the driveway, and when he turns off the car, when the hum of the engine stops, I wake up. That happens to me sometimes. Sometimes, I'll be listening to a CD, and then the CD will end, and the quiet will make me wake up.

I wake up and I'm all groggy, and I yawn and wonder what time it is.

Come on, Doreen, let's go inside, Dad says.

We get out of the car, and all the lights are off in the house, and Matthew's car isn't in the driveway anymore. I wonder if Mom and Tracey are still up, waiting for us to come back. I wonder if Matthew's hiding, if he's going to jump out from behind somewhere and try to stab Dad or something.

Dad opens the front door, and we walk inside, and all the lights are off. I guess it's kind of late. I peek into the hallway, and Mom and Tracey's doors are closed, and their lights are off. I turn to go into my room, but Dad tells me to wait.

He goes to the hall closet and pulls out fresh white sheets and hands them to me. He looks sort of embarrassed to be giving them to me.

No reason you should sleep on the bare mattress, he says, looking down.

Thanks.

Goodnight, Doreen, he says.

Goodnight, Dad.

Then he just turns around and walks into his room, and I'm just standing in the hallway, holding the sheets. As soon as his door closes, I want to bang on it and ask a million questions. Actually, I pretty much only want to ask him, What's going to happen?

I put the sheets on my bed and then I take a shower. I put it on so hot it burns my skin, but I like the way it feels. I haven't looked at my body in a long time. I have bruises and cuts everywhere, all over me, and I'm sore all over too. I stick my face up so I get the most water possible, and then I sit down on the shower floor and let the water hit me, straight on. It feels so good, just a little painful, but in the best way. I feel the scratches on my neck sting, and I feel the skin on my face get all dry and tight, and I don't know how long I stay in there, soaping and shampooing and just letting it hit me.

Then I get out and towel off a little, and I don't bother with brushing my hair. I just put on a T-shirt and underwear while I'm still wet from the shower and slip into fresh cool sheets, and I start thinking of more questions I have to ask Dad, like, Is he really going to kill Matthew? and What did Henry look like? but mostly just What's going to happen, what's going to happen? But then I sleep so long and hard and deep that I don't even dream.

A few days later I'm at Tower with Ted. I told him the whole story, except about Henry, because I don't think I want to tell anyone that. Ted's been kind of weird to me since I told him about Matthew. For a second, he couldn't say anything. He couldn't even look at me.

Did you suspect anything? I asked.

Well, I mean, I knew you kind of liked him, but . . . he said, and then he just trailed off.

Since then, since that day when all that shit happened, I haven't been grounded anymore. Mom's been teary all the time, but I think Dad calmed her down a little. Tracey's been all bratty and won't speak to me—she refuses to go out with her friends because I gave her a black eye, so she just walks around, holding an ice pack to her face, bitching. I even got relieved of garage detail. I told Dad that pit's not going to get clean until he and Mom go through boxes and decide for themselves what they want to keep. Mostly I've just been seeing Ted and hanging out like always, except that since I told him about Matthew, I think he's kind of afraid. Of what, I don't know.

The day after it all happened, Dad took the day off from work, which he *never* does, and he just hung around, talking to Mom and me. He went through a couple of hours when he was really pissed off, when he wanted to send the police after Matthew, but I begged him not to. I mean, I had a hard enough time telling Ted—I don't want to talk to a goddamn lawyer and the police and a jury and have some doctor poking at me. I watch TV. I know how it goes. Dad still might do something, though. I don't know. Tracey's tried to call Matthew a few times, and she said the phone just rings and rings. Truth is, I don't think it's worth it. Dad believes me. Ted believes me. Mom probably believes me, but that just doesn't matter as much for some reason. Who knows if Tracey believes me or not, but who cares what she thinks. I mean, really.

Me and Ted make quite a pair, though. He's got his black eye and bleedy scabs, and I've got Tracey's rat scratches all over my neck. Ted wears sunglasses and looks down when we're outside. He feels like everyone's looking at him, at us, talking about what freaks we are. And maybe they are. I think we look pretty cool. Cool and mean and like we get into fights a lot.

We go into Tower to get a CD, because we heard there was a

Pixies import they're always out of. It'll probably cost a thousand dollars, but me and Ted have decided to split it, and we'll just trade the CD back and forth between us. I mean, we're always together anyway, it won't really matter too much.

We're looking through the section we're supposed to, and we see it, and it's beautiful. Pixies, Live in France. They haven't had this in so long. I turn it over and look at the play list and it looks incredible. So much live Pixies. I almost want to scream, I'm so happy.

Let me see it, Ted says, and I hand it to him. Wow, it looks so good, he says.

He keeps talking about how good it looks and how he wants to rip the plastic off it right now, but I'm distracted, because I see this girl. Long perfect hair, skimpy halter, jean shorts.

I start to walk away from Ted, and I hear him yammering, and then I hear him say, Doreen? Doreen? But I keep walking toward the girl. I don't even know what I'm supposed to say, but I know I have to say something.

I get up close to her, right behind her, and I can smell her shampoo and lotion and makeup. She smells like flowers.

Hey, girl, I say, and I lean up against some CDs like I'm in a movie.

Alexandra Stuart turns around and looks surprised and disturbed, and then her eyes shift, and I know she's looking at my neck.

Doreen, she says, Oh my God, what happened to your neck? she says, kind of grossed-out, touching her own neck.

I got in a fight, I say, looking her over, looking at her stupid mouth hanging open.

She looks like she doesn't believe me at first, but then she looks back at my neck and winces.

So how have you been? I say, all chatty and cheery.

Fine, she says, looking weirded-out, but not scared.

Yeah? You having a good summer?

Yeah, she says quietly, and I can tell she just has no idea what to think of any of this. I mean, neither do I, really.

That's so great . . . that really is great news, I say, and I sound a little nutty.

Hey, Ted, I yell across the store, and Ted's lurking around over where the Pixies are, practically hiding his face.

He looks up all nervous, like he wouldn't mind dying right now. And I'm thinking, Come on, Ted. Go with me on this.

Look who's here, I scream, pointing at Alexandra, and everyone's looking at us, and I might as well be holding a neon sign.

Come on, come say hello, I yell.

Hey, could you keep it down, says the snotty register guy who is *so* alternative, I'm surprised he can live on the same planet as the rest of us.

I'm real sorry, I say to him. I didn't mean to make a scene.

The register guy makes a face at me, and I flip him off without looking at him, and Ted comes over, wearing his sunglasses, which cover half his face.

Doreen, stop yelling, OK? Alexandra says, all embarrassed.

Oh, OK, is this better? I whisper. You remember Ted, right?

Hey, Ted, she says, not looking at him.

Hey, Alex, Ted says, looking at the floor.

Come on, Ted, I say, all obnoxious, She can't get a good look at you with those things on. I take his sunglasses off, and I hold his face by his chin with one hand, and I feel him get hot and red, and I turn to Alexandra.

Look familiar? I say.

Now Alexandra looks pissed. Pissed because I've embarrassed her. Pissed because I even have the nerve to talk to her.

Doreen, what's your point? she says all snotty, and Ted slips away to pay for the CD.

My point is this, princess, I say, and I get all up in her face, and she doesn't look as comfortable as she did a second ago. I say, The next time your boyfriends have a problem, they can come to my house, OK?

Alexandra barely looks at me and says, You're so fucking weird.

And you're so fucking *tight,* from what I hear, I say, loudly, and she blushes bad, and the register guy looks over, and Ted's ready to go, but I turn back to Alexandra and she looks up at me, burning shame all over, and I say to her, That's what your cousin tells me anyway.

Then Ted and I turn without looking back and get out of the store and start walking really quickly.

You are nuts, Ted says, putting his sunglasses back on, and I'm just laughing.

What? You didn't like that? You didn't think that was cool? I say.

Well, yeah, he says. But now we're both probably going to get our asses kicked.

Bring them on, I say, and Ted doesn't look as excited as I do, but it's OK.

Come on, Ted, I say, all obnoxious, She can't get a good look at you with those things on. I take his sunglasses off, and I hold his face by his chin with one hand, and I feel him get hot and red, and I turn to Alexandra.

Look familiar? I say.

Now Alexandra looks pissed. Pissed because I've embarrassed her. Pissed because I even have the nerve to talk to her.

Doreen, what's your point? she says all snotty, and Ted slips away to pay for the CD.

My point is this, princess, I say, and I get all up in her face, and she doesn't look as comfortable as she did a second ago. I say, The next time your boyfriends have a problem, they can come to my house, OK?

Alexandra barely looks at me and says, You're so fucking weird.

And you're so fucking *tight,* from what I hear, I say, loudly, and she blushes bad, and the register guy looks over, and Ted's ready to go, but I turn back to Alexandra and she looks up at me, burning shame all over, and I say to her, That's what your cousin tells me anyway.

Then Ted and I turn without looking back and get out of the store and start walking really quickly.

You are nuts, Ted says, putting his sunglasses back on, and I'm just laughing.

What? You didn't like that? You didn't think that was cool? I say.

Well, yeah, he says. But now we're both probably going to get our asses kicked.

Bring them on, I say, and Ted doesn't look as excited as I do, but it's OK.

She looks like she doesn't believe me at first, but then she looks back at my neck and winces.

So how have you been? I say, all chatty and cheery.

Fine, she says, looking weirded-out, but not scared.

Yeah? You having a good summer?

Yeah, she says quietly, and I can tell she just has no idea what to think of any of this. I mean, neither do I, really.

That's so great . . . that really is great news, I say, and I sound a little nutty.

Hey, Ted, I yell across the store, and Ted's lurking around over where the Pixies are, practically hiding his face.

He looks up all nervous, like he wouldn't mind dying right now. And I'm thinking, Come on, Ted. Go with me on this.

Look who's here, I scream, pointing at Alexandra, and everyone's looking at us, and I might as well be holding a neon sign.

Come on, come say hello, I yell.

Hey, could you keep it down, says the snotty register guy who is *so* alternative, I'm surprised he can live on the same planet as the rest of us.

I'm real sorry, I say to him. I didn't mean to make a scene.

The register guy makes a face at me, and I flip him off without looking at him, and Ted comes over, wearing his sunglasses, which cover half his face.

Doreen, stop yelling, OK? Alexandra says, all embarrassed.

Oh, OK, is this better? I whisper. You remember Ted, right?

Hey, Ted, she says, not looking at him.

Hey, Alex, Ted says, looking at the floor.

He doesn't have to. I can be excited for both of us.

Ted's holding our CD to his stomach like it's our kid or something, and we head toward his house so we can listen to it all afternoon and memorize everything about it, and I bet it's going to be so good that I'll be dying to get to his house tomorrow morning, after not hearing it all night. Ted starts smoking and coughing and wheezing, and I laugh at him because he sounds like an old man, and we have to stop, and he tries to tell me something but he can't because he keeps coughing and I start laughing, and then he really can't talk because he starts laughing while he's coughing, and then he sort of gets a grip and quiets down, but I'm still standing there, laughing for no good reason like an idiot.

Like this is the only one...

Floating
Robin Troy

The Perks of Being a Wallflower
Stephen Chbosky

The Fuck-up
Arthur Nersesian

Dreamworld
Jane Goldman

Fake Liar Cheat
Tod Goldberg

Pieces
edited by Stephen Chbosky

Dogrun
Arthur Nersesian

More from the young, the hip,
and the up-and-coming.
Brought to you by MTV Books.

MUSIC TELEVISION®

POCKET
BOOKS